# Guilt by Association

*A Murder in the Mountains Novel*

*3*

Heather Day Gilbert

Guilt by Association
By: Heather Day Gilbert

Copyright 2017 Heather Day Gilbert

ISBN: 978-0-9978279-2-7

978-0-9978279-2-7
Interior Formatting by Polgarus Studio

Published by WoodHaven Press

Series: Gilbert, Heather Day. A Murder in the Mountains series; 3
Subject: Detective and Mystery Stories; Genre: Mystery Fiction

Author Information: http://www.heatherdaygilbert.com

Author Newsletter: http://eepurl.com/Q6w6X

# Other Books by Heather Day Gilbert:

*Miranda Warning,* Book One in
*A Murder in the Mountains* Series

*Trial by Twelve,* Book Two in
*A Murder in the Mountains* Series

*Out of Circulation,* Book One in the *Hemlock Creek Suspense* Series

*Undercut,* Book Two in the *Hemlock Creek Suspense* Series

*God's Daughter,* Book One in the
*Vikings of the New World Saga*

*Forest Child,* Book Two in the
*Vikings of the New World Saga*

*The Message in a Bottle Romance Collection*

*Indie Publishing Handbook:*
*Four Key Elements for the Self-Publisher*

*Dedicated to the foster and adoptive parents who've jumped through all the seemingly endless hoops and stepped into the line of fire to love and rescue the children who couldn't save themselves.*

*And to those who've given of their time and resources to create safe havens where addicts can rehabilitate and rebuild their lives.*

*The world needs more people like you.*

# Prologue

The most satisfaction I have ever experienced as a parent was to stand behind you in your successes, to watch you reach your potential. To know that on some level, you represent your family to the world at large.

But then something shifted, and you no longer wanted to spend time with your own blood. Your wayward peers stepped in, circling you like vultures, and they carried you off with them. Suddenly, you were too far gone.

I blame myself, of course. All that psychological nonsense about letting teens set their own boundaries, all those lies about giving you space to sow your oats—I can finally see through that. But it's too late. I have dropped the ball too many times. Now you've finally reappeared in our lives, but I can do nothing to protect you unless you start talking to me again.

I swear to you, I *will* make things right. Someday, you are going to stand again, and you are going to make us all proud.

But I will not count those blameless who have led you so very far astray.

# 1

"You sure you're okay with this, Tess?" My mother-in-law, Nikki Jo, pulls a red coffee cup from her cabinet. She knows how uncomfortable I am with the latest call from my mom.

"I think so. The temp agency won't mind if I take a day off, and if you don't mind watching Mira Brooke..."

Nikki Jo gives her highlighted blonde layers a violent shake and pours liberal creamer into my coffee. "Never. I always have time for your girlie. Now what's your momma need, again?"

Good question. My mom's only been out of prison three months—it took longer for her release than she initially thought—and lately, she keeps calling me up, almost as if I need to walk her through the most basic things, like how to make fried chicken, how to use a debit card to pump gas, or how to sort laundry. I know she never was a housekeeper, and I know she's been incarcerated for years, but it's like she's suffering some kind of memory loss.

Her latest request that I visit apparently stems from her attempt to buy a "real house" like mine, versus the broken-down trailer she's still living in. A good idea, since I doubt if the ramshackle abode of my childhood can make it through many more winters.

"She mentioned something about a realtor." I take a deep, invigorating slurp of the vanilla brew.

Nikki Jo pushes the basket of biscuits toward me, as well as a jar of her homemade peach jam. "I figure she's kind of at loose ends, living there all by herself, don't you?"

Nikki Jo, bless her heart, can't possibly grasp how resourceful my mom can be. Like the time she offered to babysit the neighbors' kids for extra income, then left them in my preteen hands for an entire two weeks so she could hit bars during the day.

I sink my teeth into the flaky biscuit, hoping my sour memories will float away. Mira Brooke squeals in the living room, where she's playing with my brother-in-law, Petey.

"Maybe," I mumble.

Nikki Jo leans across the table. Her hazelnut gaze flits over my face. There's something about her brown eyes, so similar to my husband Thomas', that seems to cut through my defenses and shine a light right into my heart.

She pats my hand. "I know you're nervous, hon. But Thomas said Pearletta has changed."

Whether Pearletta Vee Lilly has changed or not remains to be seen. And I really wish I didn't have to be the one to see it.

Thomas gets home at nine, just as I'm pulling on my PJs. Although we'd hoped his hours would be shorter with his new prosecuting attorney position, he's actually been staying later.

He pulls off his shirt and tie, then gives me a suggestive look and flexes his tricep.

I'm too stressed to take his hottie bait. "Hon, I'm driving over to Boone to see my mom tomorrow, so I need to get some sleep. Your food's down on the stove."

He clasps his chest. "Shot through the heart, babe. But I might survive." He strides over and strokes my hair out of my face. His strong hand presses into my lower back and he pulls me into a tight embrace. "You just smell so clean and fruity and delicious." His lips close over mine and by the time he releases me, I give a little gasp.

He gives a triumphant grin. "You were saying…?"

I sigh, dropping back into reality with a thud. "I should be back late tomorrow night. Your mom will keep Mira Brooke up there, and I'm sure she'll drop some food off for your supper. You'll just need to feed Velvet."

Hearing her name, our white kitty uncurls from the foot of my bed and curls around my leg expectantly.

"No problem," he says. "And hey, guess who I saw today?" He doesn't give me time to guess. "Detective Tucker. Or I guess you know him as *Zeke.*"

Thomas still can't believe his superhero homicide detective lets me call him by his first name.

"Well, I guess if you'd helped him catch a serial killer, he might let you call him Zeke, too."

"Very funny. And by the way, don't be doing that again."

"Not in my plans—for the rest of my life."

"Good. Anyway, Zeke said you should give him a call sometime." He heads downstairs to eat, so I snuggle under the red-and-blue star patterned quilt on our bed. Nikki Jo gave this to me—quilted by her grandmother—and every time I lie on it, I feel like I'm part of something bigger than myself. Something stable.

My drive to Boone gives me lots of time to think—too much time. As I wind through the greened-up mountains, I wish I'd loaded an audiobook to my phone. Instead, I sing my favorite hymns and mentally gear up for this meeting.

I won't go into Mom's trailer, since that's the root cause of the claustrophobic issues I have to this day. We can just head right out to look at houses, I can give some input, then I can drive home.

The scenery looks the same as always. So many houses sit on the high, cleared sides of the mountains. I hold my breath every time I pass someone riding a mower along the vertical hillside of a front yard. One modern mountainside house actually has goats lounging on the driveway, soaking up some sun.

As I get closer to Mom's, the long shadow of coal mining covers everything. Huge overhead pipes, coal tipples, and cleaning stations occur at regular intervals—some abandoned, some in use. Tops of mountains that were once scraped clean of trees for mining are now covered in low green growth. Towns are sprinkled with vacant buildings and burned-out houses.

Finally, the sign for Jasper Branch Road comes into view. It has multiple bullet holes in it, like most of the road signs around here. I've yet to figure out how people manage to position themselves on the side of the road to aim at them, much less why no one living behind the signs has gotten hit.

I pull off the main road, my SUV rattling across a board bridge that sits astride a half-dried creek. Dead ahead is a familiar rusted gate, still emblazoned with a faded sign reading *Scots' Hollow Trailer Park*.

I roll through the park, glancing around. There's a utilitarian vibe here, probably because there are no trees to break up the rows of houses. The only trees in sight edge the back of the park, near Mom's place. Most trailers are older, the same era as Mom's, but many have been spruced up with flags or decorative planters.

Although I drive slowly down the dirt lane that connects the homes, I'm forced to slam on my brakes when a small boy darts in front of me as he chases a ball. I roll down my window, hoping to stop him from doing this again.

"Hey! You need to be careful! Didn't you see me coming?"

The tow-headed child looks at me, but gives no response. Instead, he deliberately starts bouncing the neon pink ball, smacking it hard against the ground. His cheeks are dirt-smudged and his shocking blue eyes are protected by a thick line of blond lashes. His too-short shorts expose knobby knees, and he's wearing a long-sleeved shirt, which is way too hot for this weather.

Some inherent recognition stirs in me. He might be hiding bruises with those sleeves. And the way he's looking at me—like he wouldn't care if he *had* been run over—speaks louder than a verbal response ever could.

My childhood memories suck me under. While Mom never beat me, desperation and hopelessness are feelings I surely understand.

I soften my tone. "You be careful, okay? Take care of yourself."

Mom's trailer is around the next curve, so I inch toward it. In my rearview mirror, I watch the boy skitter up to a broken-down porch and drop onto the step, like the weight of the world is on his shoulders.

I rap at Mom's door, already eager to leave. The park always seems to be shrouded in shadows, both literal and figurative.

I hear her heavy shuffling and she finally opens the flimsy door. She's wearing a blue tank top and a loose floral skirt. "Tessa Brooke! Come on in and have yourself a sandwich before we go."

"Thanks, Mom, but I ate a while ago. Already had coffee, too. Didn't you say your realtor appointment was at noon?"

"More like twelve-thirty. So we have time to catch up."

That's the very last thing I want to do, since Mom has no chairs on the porch, which means we'd have to sit—

"Come on in," she repeats.

"We could just stand here and talk. It's nice out," I lie.

"What? In this heat? Come sit on the couch. Sally gave me her couch and it's practically new."

Out of excuses, I take a deep breath and follow Mom inside. Most of the furniture looks the same, but she's definitely made an effort to make the place more homey. A candle flickers on the kitchen counter and realistic silk flowers are positioned in small vases in the living room.

I settle into the new couch, which is quite upscale.

"Who's Sally again?"

She pulls her unnaturally bronze hair off her face and glances around. She finds a ponytail holder and shoves her hair through it. "Sally's a neighbor. Has a kid."

"A boy?"

Mom shakes her head. "Teen daughter—a real handful."

Anyone who is deemed "a real handful" by Pearletta Vee Lilly must be pretty far gone. I brush my overgrown, sweaty bangs out of my eyes, wishing Mom had more powerful air conditioning. The heat only adds to my irritation at the world in general for letting kids run wild. "Well, the person who has that little blond boy needs to keep better tabs on him. I nearly ran into him out there!"

"He lives with his grandma. It's sad—his momma left him for drugs. Sally thinks her girl's on them, too."

I actually *don't* want to know that drugs are still running rampant in this park. I don't want to know they've claimed more young victims, like the teen addicts my mom used to deal her prescription meds to. But at least Mom is finally talking like drugs are the enemy, so apparently her prison time wasn't in vain.

"I hate to hear that," I say.

Mom lumbers over to the kitchen. "I need to get something to eat before we go. The realtor, Samuel, will be coming to pick us up."

From her emphasis on his name, I figure she finds the man attractive. My mom finds most men attractive.

She's just whipped up a peanut-butter sandwich when her front door begins to shake with a frantic knocking.

"I'll get it," I say, hoping the little boy hasn't gotten run over. I stride over in two steps and throw the door open. "Yes?"

The man in front of me is in his forties and somewhat handsome. But his eyes dart past me, scanning the living room for something.

His words are punctuated with urgency. "You have to help. You have to call the police. Outside your trailer. There's a dead boy."

# 2

Mom shouts from the kitchen. "Samuel? What's going on?"

I yell at Mom, not even waiting to see if Samuel is right. "Call the cops!"

I shove the small man out of my way and bound down the rickety steps, scanning the front of the trailer. I see no body.

"Where—?"

Samuel leans out the doorway, pointing toward the end of Mom's trailer. I walk in that direction, hoping against hope that the realtor was mistaken and the boy is still breathing. How could the child have been knocked that far from the road? Had Samuel been racing through and hit him?

I walk across the stubby grass until I round the corner, surprised by some brilliant red-pink poppies that have sprung up near the base of the trailer. Is it possible those seed packets I planted so many years ago, praying for splashes of color in my monochromatic life, finally took root?

Breaking my preoccupation with the stunning poppies, I look at the ground. Just a few steps in front of me, a body lies face-down, but it's not the blond child. This is a teenage boy with scraggly brown hair, and it's obvious he's not breathing. His fingertips are a weird blue shade. My first thought is cyanide poisoning, but I've probably read too many mysteries. Still, there's no way his fingers are blue because he was too cold. It's pushing ninety degrees out here.

"*Mom!*" I shout.

Mom peeks around the corner, her tone strangely subdued. "I'm here. I called the police and they're on the way." She steps closer. "That looks like the boy who's been seeing Sally's daughter, Ruby, but I'm not sure."

"Just seeing her? Or do you think he's tangled up in drugs, too?"

Mom reflects a moment. She focuses on the side of the trailer instead of on the sprawled body in front of us.

"I guess he could be. Sally said they were always together these last few months. Say, you don't think the cops are going to suspect me or something, do you?"

I hedge. "They know your record, so if this ties in with drugs, they might have to follow up. But you're clean now, right?"

I tack that last question on like it's an afterthought, when really it's been my *only* thought since Mom moved back into her trailer.

Mom shrugs. "Of course. I wouldn't go back to it." She takes a glance at the boy and makes a slight gagging noise. "I'll wait inside."

As she rushes back toward the porch, I take in all the details I can. The dead teen has some serious bed-head, like he hasn't washed his hair for days. But his clothes look newer and they're clean. I'm so tempted to turn him over, but I wouldn't dare. His black flip-flops dangle loosely from his feet.

Something bright blue protrudes from under his chest. I step closer and nudge at it with my foot. It's a plastic-coated ID that's flipped face-up so I can make out his picture. I lean down and try to read the partially-hidden words.

The realtor speaks behind me and I jump. "Who is that kid?"

"I'm trying to find out."

He groans as if the whole world has let him down. "I don't know how we can stay on-schedule today if the police are coming. Your mom was hoping to look at several houses…" He raises an eyebrow, probably waiting for me to dismiss him.

"Afraid you're not going to get off so easy," I joke.

His lips pucker as he gives me a look of disbelief. Why is he so antsy to get going? I finish my thought.

"The police will want to talk to you, since you were first on the scene. Standard protocol," I explain. I don't actually know if that's the case, but it sounds about right.

As if on cue, a vehicle pulls up. It's a familiar camouflage Hummer. A half-grin pops onto my face and Samuel gives me another weird look. I ignore him and stride toward the tank-like vehicle, because I know exactly who's driving it.

My steps slow as I realize the friend I'm walking to meet is a homicide detective. Why on earth would a *homicide* detective be first on this scene? And what's he doing all the way down in Boone County, anyway?

Detective Zeke Tucker's salt-and-pepper hair is just as short as ever, and his matching beard is neatly trimmed. He looks tan and healthy, like he's been basking in the sun all summer. He's open-carrying a very substantial handgun (Thomas would call it a "hand cannon") in a leather chest holster. Even in the heat of summer, he's wearing his ever-present combat boots. I'm guessing those boots have definitely seen some combat.

His nearly-black eyes fix on me for a moment, then flick to Samuel, who seems to be hiding directly behind me.

He addresses me first. "Tess. I'd ask what you're doing here, but I know you'll ask me the same thing. Fact is, I was passing through on another case and they called me in since I was closest to the scene. I'm friends with Biff, the sheriff in this county. He wanted me to swing by and get the lay of the land."

Normally, I'd laugh at the name *Biff,* but the way Detective Tucker says it gives it all kinds of gravity.

I try to explain. "Hi, Detective"—I have to correct myself— "*Zeke.* This is my mom's place. I came to look at houses with her and this realtor, Samuel. He's the one who found the body." I step aside to fully expose the coward.

His gaze narrowing, Zeke moves toward Samuel. As he passes by me, a nearly electric charge ripples the air. Zeke carries himself like a predator you know you can never escape, so you don't even bother to try. His menacing reputation has actually inspired some criminals to confess *before* he ever appears to question them.

He glances at a notebook in his hand. "So you saw the body first? Walk me through that."

Samuel's slim hands tremble and he licks his dry lips.

Zeke just stares at him until the silence gets downright awkward.

Samuel starts jabbering. "I showed up right on time to meet Mrs. Lilly for our showing. I parked over there." He points to his older-model silver sedan, which is parked directly opposite the body. "I noticed something lying on the ground. I walked over that way and saw the kid, then I immediately went to the door and told Mrs. Lilly and her daughter to call the police."

Zeke gives a brief nod. He glances toward the side of the trailer. "Samuel, you can wait inside if you'd like, but don't leave until the police get here."

Samuel runs up the porch steps and gives a frantic knock.

Zeke starts walking, then turns briefly. "Tess, you want to come with me?"

I trail after him, once again getting distracted by the bright poppy patch. Did Mom actually plant and water those? I find it impossible to believe.

Zeke dons gloves and begins to look over the body. I give him my initial impressions, which are admittedly feeble.

But when he's finished, he straightens and looks me in the eyes. "You know, I was actually planning on calling you this week. I have a load of work coming in now that I've taken on a couple new counties. I'm an organized man, but I have a hard time staying on top of the paperwork. Would you want to be my secretary? You could just work out of my office in Buckneck, since it's close to you. I'm hardly ever in there."

Excitement races up my spine. My work as a temp has been okay because it's flexible, but it's also totally unfulfilling. I've been thinking about looking for another job, but haven't had time to get serious about it. Now, a man I highly respect has asked me to be his secretary.

"Administrative assistant." I correct the term under my breath.

He shoots me a quizzical look. "Whatever you want to call it. I can see if the department's willing to pay you, but if not, it'll come out of my paycheck. And maybe sometimes I can bounce ideas off you, if you're good with that. You have an instinct for things. Just now, you mentioned that although this kid's hair looks like he's been sleeping in a car for weeks, his clothes are well-maintained. Kid this age, maybe nineteen or twenty, is probably checking in at his parents' to get his laundry done. We need to find them."

He pulls the blue name tag up and wipes dirt from it, exposing the name. "Mason Roark. Looks like he's an assistant caregiver at someplace called Tranquil Waters. Nursing home, you think?"

"Sounds more like a funeral home," I say.

He points to me. "You have a phone? Let's Google it."

I grin at his youthful terminology, but extract my phone from my back pocket. It takes some doing, but we finally nail down what Tranquil Waters is.

Zeke whistles. "Drug rehab center, huh? And looks like it's tucked up tight in one of these hollows."

Police vehicles finally whir into view, converging outside the trailer. Samuel comes down the stairs and approaches us, an irritated look on his face.

"I've been knocking this whole time and your mother hasn't opened the door. I really need to get out of this heat." He fans at his face.

I expect Zeke to scoff and say something like, "Poor little pansy's wilting," but instead, Zeke turns to me. His look has changed.

Officers with bags and gloves walk around me, giving respectful nods to Zeke on their way to the body. A sheriff hitches up his pants and strides toward us.

I turn back to Zeke, a strange dread uncurling as I meet his gaze. I guess his next question before he voices it.

"You saw your mom go back inside?"

"I heard her head that way."

"I see two cars here—yours and that one of the realtor's." Zeke pauses for a moment. "So where's your mom's car?"

I can't stop myself. I glare at Zeke, jabbing a finger toward him. "What're you saying?"

The sheriff butts in. "Hey, you're Pearletta Vee's daughter, ain't ya? I remember your pretty face from years ago, when we had to take your momma in. Drugs, wasn't it?"

I don't answer. Instead, I race up the porch stairs and turn the doorknob, but it's locked. I pound on the door's faded varnish. "Mom! Hey, Mom, I need you to open up."

I wait to hear movement inside, but it's silent. I give a few more knocks for good measure, then speed down the steps to see if her small Kia is parked in its shady spot behind the trailer. There are weeds galore, but no car.

Zeke doggedly makes his way toward me, concern etching his face.

"She's gone." I speak the words aloud, daring myself to believe them.

"Looks like it," Zeke says.

He doesn't mention anything about my mom's history. He doesn't ask if she knew the dead teen. But he does reach out and pat my shoulder. And that's enough to rip a hole in the flimsy cushion of trust I've inflated around my heart.

Pearletta Vee Lilly is still a world-class liar.

# 3

In a fog, I follow Zeke as he briefly speaks to Sheriff Biff. They must give Samuel the okay to leave, since the realtor jumps in his car and rips out like his time is pure gold.

Zeke leads me up the steps to the porch. He tries the door again. Some part of me hopes it's unlocked, that it's all been some crazy misunderstanding.

He shakes his head slightly, then he walks down the steps. He grabs a larger rock from the yard and returns to the door, where he covertly pulls a keychain out of his pocket. I'm not sure where the rock fits into this scenario, so I keep watching.

He tries one key, but it doesn't fit. The next key slides in and he pulls it out a bit, then turns it to the right while gently hitting it with the rock. He repeats the turn/bump process and on the second attempt, the key turns and he opens the door.

"Trailer locks." He makes a disgusted face.

I'm going to pretend like I didn't see what just happened, although it could be perfectly legal for a detective to carry bump keys.

We scour the small trailer, but it's clear Mom is gone.

"Do you think she packed her things?" he asks.

I search her bedroom, but can't definitively say any of her clothes are missing. Shoot, I don't even know if she owns a suitcase.

In the bathroom, I don't see her usual razor sitting in the shower, but that could just mean she recently tossed her old one. Her bathroom mirror cabinet is always in disarray, so that doesn't give me any clues. As I examine the bottles, I'm thankful that the strongest medication I run into is Xanax.

Although I wonder when she had to get on that.

"I can't say," I shout toward the hall. I wander into the kitchen, noting she only managed to take a couple of bites of her peanut butter sandwich. I feel a ping of sadness that she's running on empty, but I shut it down. She has done this to herself.

Like always.

I fall into the soft cushions of Sally's hand-me-down couch, toying with a throw pillow. The heart-shaped pillow is so obviously Mom's addition—all silky magenta and purple swirls. It belongs in a teen girl's room, not on a couch in a living room. My heart clenches and I clear my throat, as if that will settle my tumbled emotions.

Zeke sits on a nearby chair and briskly scrubs his beard with his hand. "Any reason your mom would've had any dealings with the dead teen?"

"She didn't seem to know for sure who he was. Said he

might be dating a neighbor's daughter."

"I'll need that neighbor's name."

"Mom said her name is Sally, but you could ask the guy who owns the trailer park, Billy Jack Hopkins, for the details."

Zeke nods. "You heading back to Buckneck, now your mom's house-hunting has been cut short?"

I start to nod, but realize I can't go home yet. Not with Mom running around, who knows where. Maybe she'll come back to the trailer after the cops clear out.

"I guess I'll stick around a while."

"Sounds good. I'll give Biff your cell number, if that's okay. And you just check in with me when you're ready to get to work."

My spirits lift a bit. "I'm looking forward to it."

He grabs a scrap of paper from the counter and finds a pen. After scrawling something on it, he strides over and hands it to me. "This is the number for Biff's office. Call him if your mom shows up."

"Okay."

He peers into my eyes. "I don't have to tell you it was a serious thing for her to run away from this scene. Whether the kid overdosed or it was something else, it doesn't look good for her."

Stupid tears spring to my eyes. "I know."

He eases off. "I'll head on out—I'm sure you want to give Thomas a call."

Although many times I haven't kept Thomas fully apprised

of my comings and goings, today's events definitely warrant a call. "I'll do that, thanks. And I'm so glad you were here."

"Glad to help," he says. He opens the front door and hot, blinding sunlight pours in.

I sit in my dark cocoon of silence, feeling every bit as helpless as I did when I grew up here.

Finally, I pick up my cell phone, but it's not Thomas I call first.

"Nikki Jo? I'm going to have to stay overnight."

It takes hours, but the officials begin to clear out without asking me any other questions. I'm pretty sure Zeke told Biff and his cohorts to leave me alone.

My final sweep of the trailer ends in Mom's room. On a hunch, I pull her mattress up and whisk my hand along the top of the box springs.

It makes contact with something that I pull out. It's a green, unmarked pill bottle. When I twist the lid off, I immediately recognize the pills—OxyContin.

Disgust and fear wrestle for a moment, then I take the cowardly route I've chosen so many times before. I close the lid, shove the bottle back, and drop the mattress over it.

I'm sure the police will find it, if it comes to a full-scale search. And if that happens, I can figure out a way to explain why my fingerprints are now all over the bottle. But right now, Mom is just a witness who happened to disappear at an inopportune moment.

My conscience screams that Zeke has every right to know about those pills, especially if it turns out Mason was killed. But I can't expose Mom that way, not so soon after her release. I turned my mother in once, and I never want to do it again.

I scan the room. The brown floral wallpaper seems even darker than ever, and the walls seem to shift, like they're closing in on me. I know it's just a trick of my mind, but I bolt outside.

The sun has dropped behind the mountain and the trailer park has resumed its typical shadowy appearance. I don't glance toward the poppy-strewn edge of Mom's trailer. Instead, I stroll the other way, toward the blond boy's home. He's nowhere in sight. I pick my way around the plastic trucks and balls that litter the porch, then rap on the door.

A hunched-over, white-headed woman sticks her head out. She squints up at me, and I feel like a giant at five foot six, even though I'm fairly petite.

"What you need?"

Not your typical welcome, but I'll take it. "I'm looking for a woman named Sally. She has a teenage daughter?"

The woman grunts, chewing on something that might be tobacco. "You're wanting Sally Crump. She's a couple houses over. Number five."

"Thanks."

Her look sharpens. "Something wrong?"

Like a ray of light in the dim room, a blond head moves toward us. The little boy peeps out at me, sucking on a lollipop as big as his mouth. His lips are sticky, smeared with the blue sugar.

The grandma doesn't even pay attention to him. I have an overwhelming urge to pat his tousled head.

Instead, I voice a warning. "There was a death in the park—did you notice all the police cars?"

The old woman nods, glancing toward Mom's trailer.

I'm just getting warmed up. "With all those cars, don't you think this little scamp should stay out of the road?" I give the boy a grin, which he hesitantly reciprocates.

Grandma, however, isn't so happy. "I'll thank ye kindly to stay out of our business." She starts to shut the door in my face, but I can't stop myself.

I shove out a hand, stopping the door. I take a step toward her, taking in the smells of rotten food and mildewed laundry emanating from her trailer. "It *is* my business when your boy here nearly became a casualty in his own front yard because he was totally unsupervised."

A string of curse words flies from her lips, and the boy doesn't even flinch. His blue eyes are fixed on me as he licks the sides of his lollipop. He's heard all these words before, probably directed at him. The gist of Granny's diatribe is that unless I'm a cop or a social worker, I have no right to come up on her porch and butt into her life.

I turn, unwilling to listen to the rest of her rant. She stops yelling and slams the door behind me. As I reach the bottom stair, a small hand pats my lower leg. I look down to see the boy has trailed behind me.

"You go back home," I say. "Did you hear what I said? You

have to stay out of the road. Maybe play on the side of your house or behind it?"

He stretches his little sticky hand up in the air for me to take. A gesture of trust, bestowed so easily and quickly. Something primal rears up in me, something that wants to make sure this wordless little boy is clean and loved and safe.

His long sleeve falls back, exposing a heavy, greenish bruise on his wrist.

Fighting every instinct to march him straight out of this place, I take his hand in both of mine and lean down to his level. I throw a glance at the trailer, but the door's shut. Granny Dearest obviously ignored my advice to pay attention to this little guy.

"I have to go back to my own home soon," I explain. "But I'm going to ask someone to check in on you, okay? You just do what I said and stay out of the road."

Although he's probably four or five, he still hasn't said a word. While I don't want him to follow me to Sally's house, I still hate to tell him to go inside his dank trailer.

"Why don't you go play on your porch now? I saw you have a nice truck up there. I need to get going." I let go of his hand, which is no easy process with the lollipop goo.

He smiles wider, showing brilliant white baby teeth. He pulls his lollipop from his pocket and pops it back into his mouth like a pacifier. I wonder if that's his supper.

I take a slow breath and stand, thankful for his trusting smile.

I might not be a social worker, but I'm betting Zeke knows a good one.

# 4

Without a doubt, the number five trailer is the prettiest place in Scots' Hollow. Sally has a wraparound deck, and she's decorated it with at least six hanging ferns, which aren't cheap. Antique rocking chairs are painted bright colors, and there's an inviting mint colored metal glider that looks like it's been refurbished from the sixties. She's placed lilacs in a galvanized metal watering can for an added touch.

To all appearances, Sally has her act together.

I push the doorbell, which is in an ornate copper setting.

A woman opens the door, and I wonder if this is Ruby. She has choppy red hair, her eyes are streaked with mascara, and she's wearing a tight baby tee that says *Skateboarding is not a Crime*. I look closer, and can make out some barely-visible crow's feet and some wrinkles on her neck. Pretty sure this must be Sally.

"Yes?" She sniffs.

"I'm Tess Spencer."

She gives me a blank look, and I know what I have to follow up with.

"I'm Pearletta Vee's daughter."

She brightens a bit. "Of course! Tess! She was so excited you were coming to visit." She peers behind me. "Where is she?"

"Long story," I say. "Did the police stop by here?"

She nods. "They did. Why don't you come on in? I just made some peach sweet tea—trying to keep myself busy." She glances down at her shirt. "Oh, rats, I meant to change shirts after breakfast. All my stuff is dirty, so I grabbed one of my daughter's shirts. Then the cops came, and I totally forgot."

"Where is your daughter now? Does she know about Mason?"

"I've texted her several times, but she hasn't texted back. I have no idea where she is." She shoves a glass up to the freezer dispenser and fills it with ice, then pours tea over it and hands me the drink. "Ruby is…well, she's sort of still looking for herself."

I nod, swilling the amber nectar on my tongue. "This is wonderful tea," I say, knowing Nikki Jo would definitely approve. "Have Ruby and Mason been friends a long time?"

"Thanks. The secret is heating the peach right along with the sugar water. Anyway, to get back to your question, Ruby met Mason right out of high school last year. He'd already graduated high school a year earlier. They both took jobs at a rehab facility not far from here. *Drug* rehab, mind you. And the next thing I know, I find drugs in Ruby's purse."

"What kind?"

"Oxy."

My tea seems to curdle in my mouth, so I gulp it down. Surely my mom wasn't dealing to these kids.

Sally absently swipes beaded water from her glass, oblivious to my tortured musings. "Didn't make sense that my girl, who's never looked at drugs twice and kept a 3.4 GPA in high school, suddenly decided to start using, you know? So I figured the only new factor there was Mason." Mama Bear anger sparks her green eyes as she spits his name.

"And now Mason's dead," I add.

"Right. So I have quite a few questions to ask my daughter, if she'd ever get her fanny home. She's been out for three days."

Worry streaks through me as I start to understand. "You think something happened to her, don't you?"

She drops her gaze. "It doesn't make sense Mason was here at the trailer park without Ruby tagging along. Why did he come here by himself, when he doesn't live here? And why would he go to Pearletta Vee's place, anyway?"

I feel like a noose is tightening around my neck. Why, indeed? *There can only be one answer, Tess.*

I swig the last of the tea and come clean with Sally. "My mom ran off after she saw Mason's body," I say. "I don't know why. But would you call me if she stops in?"

Sally nods. "Sure, and I'll give you my number in case you see Ruby around."

"What does she look like?"

Sally strides over to the mantel above a faux fireplace, gingerly retrieving a framed photo of a striking, dark-haired girl

27

in a white graduation gown. She points to it with her coffee colored fingertip. "This is Ruby, but you wouldn't recognize her now. She has about seven piercings on each ear, as well as a nose ring. She's cut her hair super-short and it's purple. She wears goth makeup."

I think the correct term might be *emo* now, but I could be wrong. Petey usually keeps me apprised of such things, and it hasn't come up in our recent conversations.

"Gotcha. I'll keep an eye out, as long as I'm here." It's anyone's guess how long that will be.

"You're an angel," Sally says. "And I hope your momma shows up." Her gaze softens, as if she's doubtful that is going to happen.

A final question pops into my head as I walk down the porch steps. "Say, what do you know about that grandma in number eight? The one with the little boy?"

Sally leans against her door. "Effie Butler. That boy belongs to her son now, because the momma ran off when the kid was born. Then, three months ago, Effie's son up and moved to Alaska. Now she's saddled with caring for a kid and she's no spry fox—she's up in her eighties, I think. Sooner or later I figure he'll get shuffled off to some other family member."

We can only hope.

I wave and walk out into the falling twilight. When I pass Effie's place, there's no one outside and a light shines from a slim crack in the pulled curtains. My steps drag as I make my way to Mom's trailer. There's no car outside, so she probably hasn't returned.

As I mount the steps, a man's rumbling voice sounds behind me. "Tess?"

I whirl around, trying to pinpoint the speaker. A larger man emerges from the side of the trailer and when I see his backward baseball cap, I realize who I'm talking to.

"Billy Jack." The trailer park owner always wears his caps backward, probably trying to project a youthful vibe.

"Tess. Police came by, huh?"

"Yes." I fall silent, wishing Billy Jack might shed some light on things. I'm so worn out, I don't even bother to ask what he was doing.

He seems to register my hesitation. "Heard your momma ran."

"Yeah."

Billy Jack is the one who opened this trailer park, and he knows Mom's history as well as I do. When Mom was in prison, he didn't kick her out. Instead, he kept her trailer livable and didn't charge her a thing.

He hands me a small key ring. "Here's a spare key for the trailer. You keep it while you're here. I guess your mom took her copy."

"I guess so," I say, fiddling with the metal loop.

His voice takes on a firm tone. "Tess, don't worry about her. Pearletta Vee can take care of herself."

"I know."

He pauses, like he's choosing his words carefully. "She's changed. I know she'd do anything for that little girl of yours.

She told me she's determined to stay clean for her."

Great. Too bad that determination didn't kick in when I was a teen. But bygones need to be bygones, and I have to stop assuming Mom hasn't changed. It's entirely possible prison and rehab ended her drug habit.

"Thanks, Billy Jack. I'll be here tonight, at least."

"Stay as long as you need to. And please let me know when Pearletta Vee comes back."

"Will do."

Inside, I flip on the living room and kitchen lights. I check the fridge, hoping that part of Mom's transformation includes stocking more food than she used to. But it looks like I'm stuck with the basics.

Eggs, onions, and frozen shredded cheddar seem to provide the most viable option, so I mix up an omelet. After adding a couple slices of toast, I sit at the small table and try to piece things together in my head.

It does seem incongruous that two teens who were working in a drug rehab center got their hands on drugs. And it's also strange that Mason showed up dead outside my mom's trailer, with Ruby nowhere to be seen. Maybe I can check in at Tranquil Waters tomorrow and do a little information recon. I doubt Ruby's been showing up for work, but who knows?

After watching several episodes of *The Twilight Zone*, one of which will likely give me nightmares, I'm ready to call it a night. Thomas hasn't called yet in response to my text, but he's probably working late.

I wander into my old room, rummaging through my drawers. Sure enough, Mom kept some of my clothes. I pull out a short tee emblazoned with the Powerpuff Girls, then scrounge up some low-rider pants. After taking a quick bath, I put sheets and a blanket on my twin bed and climb in.

The trailer feels so quiet. I miss snuggling with Mira Brooke as I read her a bedtime story, listening to her happy babbling as she tries to repeat my words. Nikki Jo probably has her all tucked into the gold metal crib up at her house. Mira Brooke actually has her own room there, complete with a dangling rose color chandelier. It was a given that Nikki Jo would spoil Mira Brooke something awful, since she never had any girls of her own.

I slide my gun purse closer to the bed. My baby Glock is loaded, as usual, and tucked into the gun pocket on the side. I drop a final text to Thomas, telling him I'm pooped and we can talk tomorrow.

Thoughts tumble as I try to process the day. As I drift off, it registers that Billy Jack clicked off a flashlight after emerging from the side of the trailer. What had he been looking for?

# 5

Halfway through the night, some noise wakes me and I sit bolt upright, trying to figure out what it was. A door? No. More like a window being shoved up.

I grab the gun and tiptoe into the living room, which is so dark, I'll likely trip on something. I pause, listening for movement, but there's no sound except the whir of the air conditioner unit. The wall isn't far from me, so I back toward it, taking up a shooter stance before flipping on the light.

A slash of purple hair catches my eye, only partially hidden behind a chair.

I lower the gun. "Ruby?"

The teen peeps out at me, her eyes rounding as she sees the gun. But her reply has an accusatory edge. "How do you know who I am?"

"Why are you in my mom's trailer?" I counter.

She sweeps her purple bangs from her face. "You're Pearletta Vee's daughter? As it happens, your mom and I are friends."

"Yeah, right. I'll bet. Why don't you tell me the truth?"

"It is the truth! Me and her have been talking about stuff."

I cringe at her bad grammar, mostly because I'm betting she knows it's incorrect. "What kind of stuff?"

"I'm not answering your questions. Where is she?"

"Pearletta Vee isn't here right now. She took off for parts unknown. But your mom is looking for you, young lady."

Did I just say *young lady*?

Ruby slowly stands. Her outfit is entirely black—black ripped jeans, black T-shirt and boots, and a black leather cuff that has metal studs sticking out of it. Chains connect the cuff to the black leather bands around each finger.

Her black eyeliner and lipstick have smeared, giving the impression she hasn't cleaned her face in days.

My motherly instinct takes over. "Sit down and have something to eat."

Shockingly, she obeys without question.

My adrenaline is super-charged, but I brew a small pot of coffee just to make sure my brain is functioning properly. I cook a small egg and cheese omelet for Ruby, and she picks at it, eating only about a third. Maybe she doesn't like eggs. As she drinks her coffee, I try to come up with a gentle way to broach the topic of Mason.

Unable to think of anything, I decide to plunge right in with questions. "Do you have a boyfriend?"

"None of your business." She gives a long yawn.

"I heard you and a guy named Mason were tight."

"Yeah. Who wants to know? And why'd you say 'were'?"

33

She hasn't heard. I sit down next to her. "Ruby, there's something you need to know, but it's hard. I know you're tough, though."

She nods, eyes wide. I'm reminded how young she really is.

"Mason died. I don't know when he died, or how, but we found him near the trailer."

Her eyes harden and I can almost see the defensive walls going up. "So?"

"So, what do you think he was doing here? And don't try to tell me he was 'friends' with my mom, too."

"He wasn't. Anyway, he lives over on Beaver Point Road. He only comes here to see me."

"And where have you been hanging out lately?"

Her face turns stony. "Why should I tell you?"

Anger flashes through me. "Because my mom might be in trouble, that's why. If you really *are* her friend, you might try to help me clear her name."

"What, they think she had something to do with Mason's death? That's ridiculous."

"Why so ridiculous?"

"Because Mason didn't like her. You know why? Because she was telling me to stay away from him. So there's no reason he would've been hanging around her trailer. He didn't want to talk to her."

I take a split second to appreciate the fact that Mom was using her time to counsel a troubled teen, then I repeat my question. "Where have you been, though? Was he with you for a while?"

"You really wanna know? I quit working and I've been sleeping in my car, since I didn't want to go home."

"But why not? You have a lovely home." I think of all the times I wanted to run away from the confines of this very trailer, mostly because there wasn't a sense of *home* about it. But Sally's obviously an attentive and caring mom.

Ruby glares at me. "Yeah, I know. It's lovely."

I don't know if she's insinuating her home life isn't what it seems, or if she's acknowledging I'm right. Even though I speak sarcasm fluently, this girl is hard to figure out. And I get the feeling she's hiding something...

I look at her, more closely this time. She looks a little green around the gills and she's gripping her stomach. She didn't eat much at all. She's been yawning furiously ever since she got here. As she wipes her runny nose, yet again, on a napkin, all the pieces fit into place.

"You're coming off drugs," I say.

"Whatever."

"And you didn't want your mom to know, so you stayed away. What about Mason? Was he trying to get clean too?"

She laughs. "Not him. He even drove on the juice."

"How did he ever get a job at the rehab?"

"He wasn't using then. At that point, he said he wanted to help others get past it, like he had. It was only during this past month he'd been using. And since he wasn't stingy with his stuff, I helped myself a little."

"What was it?"

She shrugs, and her shirt inches down her shoulder. "I'm not telling you. That's like a confession or something."

"Fine. You can tell my police detective friend. I'm sure he'll be *very* interested."

She gives me a hateful look. "A few pills and a little heroin. It was no biggie, okay?"

All the more reason to get her home tonight. "Your mom's worried out of her mind, now that Mason's dead. You should at least check in with her."

"I know, I know. She was leaving all kinds of messages on my phone, but my battery died and I didn't have my charger cord." She dry-heaves as if she's going to vomit. "Fine. I guess I'll go home for now, but I'll probably need some help, because I'm not feeling really steady. Oh, and will you let me know when your mom comes back?"

She's the third person today who's asked me to do that.

I make a demand of my own. "If she comes back, I'll give your mom a call, so you'll have to stay home a while."

Ruby's mouth gapes open in yet another yawn, as if she's lost the will to fight me. "Yeah, whatever."

"Speaking of calling, I'm going to text your mom and let her know we're coming over now. Would she read it at this time of night?"

"Yeah, she'll hear the text tone. She told me she was keeping her ringer on high so she wouldn't miss my next text." Ruby actually has the good sense to drop her head in shame after admitting this.

I run into my room and grab my Glock. In the living room, I open my purse and unzip a sturdy interior pocket. I slide the gun into it. Ruby's eyes are wide as I sling the leather straps of the bag over my shoulder. "Just in case—I mean, it *is* the middle of the night."

Ruby sighs, and I lock the door behind us as we walk down the porch stairs. Billy Jack has installed three large post lights in the trailer park. Yellowy light flickers over us, making our movements look like something out of a bad horror flick.

Ruby falls behind, her steps sluggish, as if she's ready to tumble over. I pray her mom can figure out the best way to detox her girl. Maybe Tranquil Waters will give Ruby some kind of deal for switching from the working end of things to the treatment end.

Sally answers the door on the first ring, her hair backlit like she's wearing a fuzzy red halo. She takes one glance at me, then catches sight of Ruby, who's making little gagging noises.

I step aside and Sally sweeps Ruby into her arms, hugging her with that fierce, unstoppable, always-forgiving mother love. I can barely squeeze words out, but manage, "She's in drug withdrawal."

Sally nods, tears running down her face. It's obvious she's just relieved her daughter is alive.

I try to imagine my Mira Brooke as a teen, getting lured into drugs by some boyfriend. I know exactly what I'd want to do to that guy, although Thomas would probably get there first. But I can't see that we'd go as far as murder, and I doubt Sally would, either.

I glance around, now able to make out the greenish haze of trees on the mountain. Dawn is coming before long, and I have to get some sleep. And copious amounts of coffee, which is the one thing Mom seemed to stock in abundance.

"See you later." I know it's not the most poignant thing to say, but I'm too exhausted to come up with something better. I turn and walk back toward the trailer, one hand resting on the purse pocket where my Glock sits. It'd be easy for someone to get the jump on me, even with the flickery lights. There are plenty of dark corners.

My steps slow as I near Mom's porch, because I can make out the shape of a car in her driveway. A barely discernible glow shines from a crack in the tightly pulled curtains, but I thought I'd killed all the lights when I left.

I tiptoe up and try the door. It's still locked, but that doesn't mean someone didn't pop in through the window like Ruby did. I pull the gun and slowly unlock the door, easing my way in as I flick on the living room light.

A feather could knock me over when my eyes clap on someone walking down the dimly-lit hallway, just as casually as you please.

My mom.

This night is never going to end.

# 6

Mom ignores the incredulous look I must be wearing. She drops the suitcase she's lugging behind her and comes toward me. I slide the Glock back into its holster before leaning into Mom's cushy frame for a hug. No matter how many times she has let me down, she will always smell like my mom—some mix of body lotion, cigarette smoke, and coffee.

She strokes my hair from my face. "Honey, I'm so sorry I left you like that, but I'm glad to see you stuck around."

I pull back. "Why *did* you leave?"

She gives a rueful shake of her head, picking up her suitcase and dragging it over to the door. Apparently she's not ready to explain her abrupt leave of absence.

"Mom, it's the middle of the night. What are you doing?"

She puts a hand on her hip. "I guess I should ask what *you* were doing, traipsing around at night."

"Ruby came here. I took her back to her mom's."

Mom's blue eyes widen. "Poor kid."

"She said you tried to get her to break it off with Mason."

"I did, for what it was worth." Mom gives me an intense look and shifts gears. "Tessa Brooke, I need you to listen up. I can't stay here. I know those cops are going to find out Mason overdosed—I've seen it before. They're going to try to say he got his drugs from me. I'll tell you right now, I *did not* give that boy drugs. You have to believe me."

"Mom, I found—"

"Don't interrupt. I don't have time to waste. I know I'll be prime suspect number one. That sheriff has been all over my case from day one."

I stay silent, knowing that all those years ago, Sheriff Biff had only showed up because I'd turned Mom in. I pace away from her in an attempt to burn off energy I wish I didn't have this time of night.

She continues, talking to my back. "I just came back to pick up a few things; no time to hang around. But I promise you I'm innocent, baby. Don't you forget it."

She might be protesting too much. I turn around to face her. "Where will you go?"

She nonchalantly flutters her hand, her sparkly, chipped nail polish catching the light. When will she get the chance to paint her nails again?

She gives a low chuckle. "Now, don't you worry your pretty head about it. Your old momma still has some allies. And a little cash, too." She walks back into the bathroom, then emerges with a container of hair gel. After unscrewing the lid, she pulls out a wad of cash. She always did find interesting places to hide her money.

40

"Gotta go, babe. Just don't give up on me, okay?" She leans in for one more hug, then grabs her suitcase.

I reluctantly open the door for her, then follow her onto the porch. Her shadowy form disappears into the car, and she pulls away with no lights on.

Did that really just happen? Am I asleep?

I step back inside, stumbling over the doorstop. My toe starts throbbing as I lock the door behind me. Blast. I'm definitely awake.

I continue my stumbling, sleep-deprived gait down the hallway, then fall into my bed. *If* by some chance my mom isn't stringing me along like she's always done, *if* she's actually telling the truth, I'm going to have to start digging for answers tomorrow.

Sunlight peeks through the blinds and I groan. Tomorrow's already here.

Somehow, I manage to sleep until seven-thirty in the morning, when the *Law and Order* theme song sounds on my phone, letting me know it's Thomas.

"Yo," I say.

"YOLO," he responds, parroting Petey's favorite acronym for *You Only Live Once.*

The sound of his rich voice floods right through me, giving me more than a pang of homesickness. "How's Mira Brooke doing?"

"Just had breakfast up at the big house—Mom made

pancakes. Mira Brooke can now say 'pancake.'"

"Aw! I can't believe I missed it!"

"Yes, and she said it numerous times, since she was putting the chocolate chip ones away like she had a hollow leg." He laughs. "But how are things going there? Mom told me a little, and I read your text, but I don't really understand what's happening. What does Detective Tucker have to do with your mom?"

I stand and stretch, then head into the kitchen to brew some coffee. "Long story. I'll try to condense, so hold on to your hat." I launch into a brief recount of the previous day's events, although I leave out Grandma Dearest and her sad blond foundling from next door. I end by describing Mom's surprise reappearance in order to clear her as-yet-unsullied name.

Thomas seems remarkably quiet as I speak, and when I stop talking, his reaction isn't what I'd expected. His voice is firm. "I think you should stay there a little."

"What?"

"Tess, I'm not completely dense. I can read between *your* lines fairly easily, believe it or not, and I can tell you want to stick around to help your mom. There's nothing wrong with that. It's called family loyalty."

I fall silent.

He continues. "I know you haven't had a lot of respect for your mom over the years—who could blame you? But I feel like there's something bothering you about this teen's death. I mean, why was he outside your mom's trailer? Makes no sense."

Peaceful contentment floods me as I picture Thomas, sipping his creamy coffee at the table. Velvet is likely sitting on his lap, enjoying an ear rub. Thomas might be checking the internet for the morning's news, his long, tan fingers tapping impatiently at the screen. He should probably get in the shower, but he's stalling because he'd rather talk with me.

I want to reach through the phone and kiss him. Sometimes, my husband knows me better than I know myself.

A thought strikes me. "I forgot to tell you that Zeke— Detective Tucker—asked me to be his administrative assistant. I could work right at his office in Buckneck, not far from you."

There's a pause. For a split second, I fear Thomas will say I shouldn't take the job.

Finally, he responds. "Sounds like something you'd like."

"It is!"

"But I know you, babe. Answer the phones, enter the data, and file things...but don't read the reports. You can't right all wrongs."

"Of course I know that," I say. "Love you. You'd better get ready for work."

After making liberal kissy noises, Thomas says goodbye. I reflect on what he said. I can't right all wrongs, for sure. That's God's job. But I can definitely right some.

And it seems like looking into Mason's untimely death would be a great place to start.

# 7

Since I know it'll be impossible to get back to sleep, I jump in the shower, blow dry my hair into some semblance of order, and get dressed in yet another college outfit. In my wide-leg pants and mauve silk blouse, all I'd need is a chic head scarf to look like I stepped right out of Season One of *Gilmore Girls*. I'll need to hand wash yesterday's outfit, since Mom uses the Laundromat and I don't want to take time to mess with that. Or maybe Sally has some clothes I could borrow, since she's about my size.

I skip checking the fridge. It'll be easy enough to hit McDonald's for a breakfast biscuit en route to my first destination of the day: Tranquil Waters.

The trailer park is quiet and foggy as I pull out. I pray for the blond boy and for Ruby as I pass their respective homes, hoping their lives begin to look up.

It takes me an hour to get to Tranquil Waters, mostly because my phone signal keeps dropping at critical junctures. After taking two incorrect back roads, I backtrack and finally catch sight of a leaf-draped sign for Vance Hollow. There's a yellow Dead End sign tucked right behind it.

The one-lane road is paved, but it's extremely narrow. I drive along the right edge, but when a car comes barreling down in the opposite direction, I hold my breath and inch over a bit more to avoid a collision. If my tires drop off the steep side, I'll get stuck in the ditch.

First challenge in checking into rehab here: survive the driveway.

Finally, the road opens up, spilling onto a roundabout drive in front of a long ranch-style brick building. A blue sign says *Tranquil Waters* in the same white cursive lettering that was on Mason's name tag.

I open the French doors and walk up to the check-in, still mulling over what approach to take. When a brunette woman in pink scrubs opens the window, I make a quick decision.

"Hi. I was close to Mason Roark, and I wondered if I could talk to the person in charge about him?"

It's literally true. I *was* very close to Mason when he was lying outside my mom's trailer.

"Oh, I'm so sorry," she says. She has a round face and the compassionate expression of someone who could be trusted with your deepest secrets. "Director Stevens just told us all this morning. Are they planning a wake, do you know? I can't always take off during the day, but I really wanted to pay my respects. Mason was a sweet kid."

That wasn't the impression Mom and Ruby gave me, but

then again, Ruby did say he managed to hide his addiction well. Still, to hide a drug habit at a rehab facility must've been well-nigh impossible.

Or maybe someone was aware of Mason's problem and didn't tell for a reason.

The friendly woman babbles on. "I'll take you back to Director Stevens' office." She comes out from behind the desk and leads me down a wide hallway. "Mick Stevens has been here since the very start. His dad opened this place ten years ago, and when he passed, Mick took over. He's very forward-thinking. He was one of the first in the state to start using Vivitrol to help in the recovery process."

"Vivitrol?"

She stops at the last room on the right and knocks on the door, which has a nameplate emblazoned with *Director Stevens*. "Yes, it's an opioid-blocker that we use in conjunction with counseling to wean people off drugs."

"Come in," someone shouts from inside.

She swings the door open, speaking to the man with the gray brush cut behind the scuffed brown desk. "I have someone here to talk to you about Mason, Director. Her name is—?"

I rush to fill in the blank. "Tess Spencer."

The cherubic woman smiles. "I'm Lacey. Be sure to stop by the front desk before you go."

"Will do."

Lacey pulls the door shut behind her, and Director Stevens returns my interested gaze. With his military bearing and his tattooed forearms, I'm betting he was in the armed forces. "Nice to meet you, Miss Spencer."

"Missus," I correct. As usual, I forgot to put my wedding band on. It's gotten a bit tighter since Mira Brooke's birth and I haven't made time to get it resized.

"And how do you know Mason?"

I'm tempted to tell a lie, since I've already fudged my way in here. However, I have a feeling my sins will find me out.

"To tell the truth, I'm looking into Mason's death and I had a few questions."

His bushy eyebrows raise. "You're a detective?"

I give a nervous laugh. "No, no. Nothing of the sort. Although I am working for a detective. But that's not the point."

He leans forward on bulky forearms, making me feel exceptionally small and weak. "And what is the point, Mrs. Spencer?"

I don't like feeling weak, so I go on the offense. "The point is that Mason was using drugs. But he was working at a drug rehab clinic. It doesn't add up."

I expect a vociferous denial that such things could occur, but Mick Stevens surprises me.

He gives a slow nod. "It's a hole in our application process. Our employees have to allow for a criminal background check, but teens can fall through the cracks since their review process isn't as rigorous. Up until now, I haven't required mandatory drug screens due to state laws, but now that the Safer

Workplace Act has passed, I have more freedom and I'm going to start testing every job applicant."

"Sounds like a plan." I slide into my questions, hoping he'll continue to be open with me. "Do you know if Mason had any close friends here besides Ruby?"

Mick gives me a sharp look. "So you know Ruby, too?"

"My mom lives near her."

"Do you happen to know why she hasn't shown up for work this week? She's about to lose her job."

"It's not my place to say. You need to call her mom—Sally Crump." I give him Sally's number.

"Thanks. Now, I think it's best if you leave, Mrs. Spencer. I've already talked with the police about this, and I'm not really clear what your role is here."

Neither am I.

He stands, and I follow suit. I shake his extended hand. "Thanks for your time, Mr. Stevens. I can see myself out."

As I walk back down the hallway, I glance into a room with an open door. It looks homey, with a regular bedspread on the bed and a cozy lounge chair in the corner. I pass a larger room where residents are gathered in a circle, eating some kind of pastries and having an intense discussion. I'd guess at least a third of them are under age thirty. I should suggest that Sally try to get Ruby in here.

I round the corner and stop by the desk to say goodbye to Lacey, but she's nowhere in sight, so I take a seat in the upscale lobby to wait for her. The ivory and turquoise color scheme seems to whisper of relaxing beaches, and an indoor waterfall tumbles into a small koi pond. Tranquil Waters, indeed.

The doors open and someone strides in—a very tall someone—carrying a show-stopping bouquet. Lime slices line a tall, clear vase filled with pink and white peonies. Other green and pink touches add to the overall effect that this arrangement was concocted in some kind of fairyland.

His face is hidden behind the flowers, but the moment I catch a glimpse of his white-blond hair, my suspicions are confirmed. I know who this unusually gifted florist is.

I'm tempted to walk up and say hello, but it will actually be more interesting to find out what he's up to. I dip my head behind a magazine and covertly watch his every move.

Axel Becker rings the bell. It takes a couple of minutes, but Lacey finally emerges, and the smell of a hot pocket drifts into the lobby. Axel falls into an easy conversation with her, then he takes some kind of payment and picks up the vase. Carrying it to the weathered wooden coffee table in front of me, he arranges it on top of a linen runner.

The moment he glances my way, I pull the magazine higher to cover my eyes. But it's too late. I hear his steps and suddenly he's right in front of me, gently pushing my magazine down with his huge hand.

I meet his pale blue eyes.

"Tess? You are here?"

I shrug. "And so are you. You're quite a long way from your shop in Point Pleasant, Axel."

For once, the man who'd stalked me in college seems at a loss for words. Thomas is convinced Axel moved to Point Pleasant under the guise of a flower shop owner to prolong his stalking ways, but I'm ninety-five percent sure that's not the case.

It's that five percent that makes me uneasy every time Axel shows up.

Although this has to be a coincidence—he already had the flower bouquet made up, and he's obviously met Lacey before. Yet why would he drive so out of the way to make a personal delivery?

I'm not going to ask. Instead, I stand up, feeling about four feet tall next to the German giant. I pick up my purse, appreciating the familiar heaviness of my concealed gun. It's comforting to know I'm never totally on my own, no matter what I step into. I have God and I have my Glock.

Axel doesn't move, so I brusquely step around him. "I'm sort of in a hurry," I say.

He follows me, scattering koi as we breeze toward the door. "You are here for a purpose? Perhaps a visit?"

"Perhaps," I say enigmatically.

He takes two huge steps and successfully blocks my exit. "Or perhaps you are looking into something? A death, *vielleicht?*"

I narrow my eyes. "What would make you say that? And you need to move out of my way."

He acquiesces, allowing my continued retreat out the French doors. His van, emblazoned with the Fabled Flowers logo, sits parked in the turnaround. He's left the sliding door open, and I'm shocked to see his adorable assistant sitting inside. She is Asian, and as petite and dark as Axel is tall and light. I wonder if they're an item. They'd make one of the most beautiful couples I have ever seen.

He gives her a slight nod, pulling the door shut before I can even say hello.

"Jeepers," I say.

He cocks his head as if he hasn't heard that term before. "You are irritating?"

I can't help but laugh. "I think you mean *irritated*. No, Axel, I just wanted to say hi to your assistant—it's polite."

"Polite. *Ja*."

I can tell our conversation is quickly deteriorating, as he's getting more and more German with every second.

"Good to see you. *Gut*. I need to get home."

"You are returning to Buckneck?"

"*Nein*." Hang it, he's made me revert to my college German. "I'm around here for a while."

"Your daughter, she is healthy?"

"Yes." I shift on my feet, certain his assistant doesn't appreciate being left alone in the stuffy van.

"And your *Mutter?*"

My mother? How does he know about her? What does he know? Maybe he's doing flowers for Mason's funeral and he heard his body was next to Mom's trailer? But how would he know my mom's name?

Wait. He's probably talking about Nikki Jo. I'm sure I've mentioned her before to him, and everyone knows her. I'm just being paranoid.

"She's fine, too." I start to walk away.

"*Halt!*"

I come to a dead stop.

He looms up behind me. His massive presence is either sheltering or dangerous; I'm not certain which. After fishing a business card from his shirt pocket, he finds a pen and scrawls a number on the back. When I reach for the card, he presses it into my hand.

He leans down a bit toward my face, taking me right back to our college days when he leaned down after our first introduction and stole a kiss on the green.

But he's dead serious as he speaks. "Call this number if ever you are overcome."

He turns and heads back to his van, where his assistant has moved up to the passenger seat. Axel climbs in the driver's side, revs the engine, and drives off at a clip that's way too fast for a one-lane road.

I shake my head. It's anyone's guess what on earth he meant. Was he hitting on me? It didn't feel like it. It felt like he was saying he'd be around if I got into trouble, which admittedly happens now and then.

I tuck the card into my purse and take a final look at the place where Mason worked. Director Stevens seemed honest enough, but I can't shake the feeling there's something funky going on at Tranquil Waters. I need a way in—a way to gather information firsthand.

I slide into my SUV and set my purse on the floor as I work through possibilities. Charlotte isn't in the country; she's leading WVU students on an Art History tour in Europe. That leaves one friend…a dramatic, persuasive friend who's done a little snooping for me before.

I pull out my phone and call Rosemary Hogan.

# 8

Rosemary's voice is groggy. "Tess?"

"Were you asleep? It's nearly noon."

"Well, a happy hello to you, too. And for your information, yes, I was asleep. I was up late dumping someone."

I roll my eyes. Rosemary's a regular bombshell, in the most literal sense of the word. She blows up easily and the shrapnel ain't pretty, from what I've seen. It'll take a really special man to figure out how to handle the likes of her.

"I'm sure the guy you dumped is going to have a rough day, too." I glance at the yard next to the main building. There's a good-sized net there and several residents seem to be setting up a volleyball game. "Listen. You've helped me out before when I needed information—"

"Yes! When you go all Nancy Drew!"

I sigh. "Whatever you want to call it. Anyway. I have a really big job for someone. It'll require taking maybe a week off work? Do you have that kind of time, or would you even be interested?"

Rosemary guffaws. "Girl, I hardly ever miss work, so I have some serious vacation time coming. And you know I can't resist a challenge. Count me in."

"They're going to have a couple of openings for caregivers at this drug rehab place in Boone County. I need you to land one of those jobs and check into things for me."

I have no doubt that Rosemary can land any job she wants. She can look very alluring when she wants to, like Marilyn Monroe. Only this Marilyn might run you over with her truck if you get on her bad side.

"Got it. Where do I stay?"

I hadn't thought that far ahead. The idea of Rosemary squeezing into Mom's trailer with me, chain smoking every chance she gets, isn't appealing in the least. I'm not sure if it's even worth it. It *is* possible Mason just overdosed while hanging out in the trailer park.

But he was right next to Mom's trailer, and I need to know if she was involved, for my own peace of mind.

I give Rosemary directions to Mom's trailer, then throw in an additional request. "Could you bring me some clothes from my house? I'll text Thomas to get some together. I don't have time to do laundry here and what I have is"—I glance down at my elegant blouse—"dated."

"Sure. Or I could bring you some of my things?"

Oh mercy, no. Visions of tight pencil skirts, leopard prints, and *Pretty Woman* thigh-high boots flash through my mind. "I don't think you're my size. I'll just stick with my own stuff, but thanks."

We finalize details, then I start to back out. Someone raps on my window and I jump.

Lacey stands outside, a bright smile on her face. I roll down the window.

"Mrs. Spencer. I just wanted to apologize if the director was a bit…abrupt. The police questions really wore him out, and he feels terrible that he didn't see the signs that Mason was using. This death really hit him hard."

"I'm sure. He was just a kid, really."

She bobs her head. "Right. And since Director Stevens' son died so young—also of an overdose—it brings back all those memories."

That is an interesting fact. "No need to apologize. It's a tragedy, and I'm sure we're all reeling."

Her smile is back in place. "Thank you for stopping by."

As I drive down the winding road, thinking of Mason and the director's son and countless other kids from this state who've died because of drugs, anger swells. Who's supplying these teens, giving them a death sentence by turning them into young addicts?

A slithery voice echoes in my head. *Your mom did.*

Yes, she did. But she says she's not doing it now.

If only I could see her again, I could ask if she had a supplier and give his name to the sheriff.

Where would Mom go to hide out? She said she still has "allies." I'm hoping that doesn't mean she ran straight back to the dealers, because I can't think of any close friends she'd have around here. Or maybe she made friends in prison? I could call and ask…

I'm going down rabbit trails. I need to focus on the issue at hand—Mason and who he knew. As I pull into the grocery store parking lot, I plan the rest of my day. I'll pick up some flowers for Ruby, then casually ask her where Mason's family lives. I can drive over and give them flowers, too, and hopefully ask a few questions about who his friends were.

Fresh motivation fuels me and I turn to lock my car. I feel someone walk up behind me and I put my hand in my purse's gun pocket, then whirl around.

Sheriff Biff gives me a knowing smile. "Aware of your surroundings. That's good. Happened to see your car and wanted to let you know that if you see your mom, you're going to need to tell her to come down to the station. It was an overdose, but not your typical overdose."

"What do you mean? Why would Mom need to talk to you about it?"

"Let's just say someone gave him tainted drugs and we need to figure out who."

"Tainted drugs? Was it a bad batch? So more people will turn up dead?"

"That's what you'd think, isn't it? But this seems a bit more targeted." He looks down at his feet, then back at me. "So we'll need to talk with Pearletta Vee, since Mason was found right outside her trailer."

"I understand." Only too well. I know I won't get any more

info from the sheriff, but maybe Zeke could fill me in on what they found.

The sheriff tips his hat. "You have my number, right?"

"Sure do, thanks."

"Holler at me later, then," he says, ambling off to his car.

Oh, I wish I could holler, all right. At the top of my lungs.

Because as much as I want to believe my mom's not involved in this tragedy, I have the creeping feeling she is.

# 9

Back at the trailer, I check my texts. Thomas has texted once, and so has Nikki Jo. I pull up hers first, knowing there will be at least a couple of auto-correct errors that'll crack me up. I've decided Nikki Jo never, ever takes time to read over her texts before sending them.

> *Mira Brooke is having the time of her life, so don't you worry I've bit. Petey bought her some Legis with his own money, and she lived building with him. I hope you aren't feeling too loners down there. your temp agency called and I told them you were out of town, but you might want to call them back. I'm feeding Thomasband he certainly won't waste away. Love you!*

It's nice to get a little taste of home, garbled as it may be. I'm pretty sure Petey bought Legos for Mira Brooke, but for all I know, there's some new toy called Legis that I'm unaware of. I pull up Thomas' text, and it's loaded with the kind of innuendo that lets me know, beyond doubt, he misses me.

I dive into my fresh pile of groceries and fix a tuna sandwich with lettuce and tomato, accompanied by a glass of chocolate milk. Refreshed, I grab the dark red rose bouquet I'd chosen for Ruby, as well as a mixed flower bouquet for Mason's family, and head out to the car.

As I pass the little boy's trailer, I catch sight of him playing on the porch. Maybe he's heeded my advice to stay out of the road. I wave, and he gives a half-hearted wave in return.

Sally opens the door and gushes over the flowers. "I'll give them to Ruby. She's been sleeping odd hours, but I called the rehab place where she worked and they gave me some ideas of how to help her. Apparently, she's only having mild withdrawal symptoms, which probably means she hadn't been using heroin for long."

She frowns, and I know she wishes Ruby had never gotten hold of heroin in the first place.

"I wondered if you or Ruby could tell me where Mason's family is? I wanted to offer my condolences and give them some flowers."

"Oh, sure. They live right off Route 3, down Beaver Point Road. I'll write down the directions. That's mighty nice of you to do."

Mighty nosy would probably be more accurate, but I smile as if it's the least I can do.

Mason's family lives in the kind of well-kept older home that speaks to a solid upper middle-class status. I'm reminded that heroin and prescription meds have sifted into every layer of society, wrecking the lives of affluent housewives just as quickly as they tear away trailer park kids' futures.

Mrs. Roark opens the door. Although her face is puffy and blotchy, as if she's had a recent cry, she's wearing a skirt and dress shoes. I forgot to ask Sally about the wake and funeral, and I'm hoping I haven't barged in at a horrible time.

"I'm so sorry to bother you, Mrs. Roark." There's no polite way to phrase what I need to say next. "I was in the trailer park where they found Mason, and I just wanted to let you know that we're all so sorry." I awkwardly thrust the bouquet toward her, and she gives a tepid smile.

"Thank you, my dear. They're lovely."

Now what? I can't very well say I'm looking into Mason's death and casually ask if she knows any of his dealer friends' names.

She gives me one of those *Are we done here?* looks and begins to close the door.

I take a step closer. "I just wondered if Mason was commuting from here to Tranquil Waters. I mean, that's kind of a drive."

She gives me a quizzical look.

I try to explain. "I'm friends with Sally Crump, and I know Ruby had been away from home for a few days before they found Mason, so I just wondered if they had been together."

Her face hardens. "No. Mason wasn't allowed to hang around with that girl—she was bad news. He went to bed here that night."

"Oh, of course. I'm so sorry to bother you. I'll be praying for you and your family." *And trying to figure out why someone deliberately gave your son tainted drugs.*

As I walk across the tree-lined street to get into my SUV, it strikes me as odd that Mrs. Roark thought Ruby was bad news. From what Sally, Ruby, and my mom said, Mason was the one supplying Ruby with drugs.

But someone had to be supplying Mason.

If he was living with his parents and he went to bed at home that final night, how'd he wind up dead in a trailer park thirty minutes away?

As I settle into the seat, I call Zeke, planning to come clean and let him know my mom stopped in to proclaim her innocence.

His confident voice fills the line. "I'm actually over at Biff's office now. Could we meet up, maybe at that diner—what's it called? I'm starving."

"Jerry's." One of the few memories I have of my dad was at that diner. It was past my bedtime, and he took me there and bought me a meal, even though I was too small to make a dent in the burger and fries.

"That's the one. Can you meet me in thirty minutes?"

I sink into the green vinyl bench in a corner booth, ordering a coffee with two creams and sugars while I wait for Zeke to arrive. The diner is dead at this hour, except for a couple of older men who are sipping coffee and staring at me.

I finally smile and nod their way, and they turn back to their conversation. I might not be a local anymore, but I can still act like one.

When Zeke walks in, conversation stops and the coffee-swigging men have nothing but respectful glances and nods for him. I find it hilarious that Zeke has that effect on most people, but I'm kind of immune to it.

He slides into the seat opposite me, then waves the waitress down and asks for the biggest burger they have on the menu.

He eyeballs my coffee. "Aren't you hungry?"

"Nope. Already ate lunch."

"Okay. Let's get down to business. First, I've cleared you to work with me. So let me know when you're ready to show up at the Buckneck office, and I'll drop by and explain how my things are organized."

"Sounds good." I feel another little thrill that I'll be working with a police detective. "I don't know when I'll be heading back. Kind of depends."

He leans in. "You digging up anything?"

Obviously he knows me well. "Not much, and not fast, but I do have an obligation to tell you that my mom showed up in the middle of the night. She came to get some of her things, and she told me she had nothing to do with Mason's death. And is it an overdose, or are they calling it murder? Biff said something about the tox screen? I remember Mason's fingers were blue and I wondered if that was a sign of cyanide or something?"

He drowns a fry with ketchup. "Tox screen isn't back yet, but they're pretty sure what he overdosed on wasn't pure heroin. Most likely it had something laced in that made it fatal." He munches pensively. "Have you heard anything about the 2016 rash of heroin overdoses in Huntington? They figured out an elephant sedative, carfentanil, had been mixed in. Users are demanding a bigger bang for their buck, and strong sedatives like Fentanyl can give that effect, at the risk of killing people. Fentanyl is 100 times more potent than morphine. Another drug they'll sometimes cut in is Xanax."

I take a gulp of lukewarm coffee, trying not to picture that bottle of Xanax in Mom's medicine cabinet.

He continues. "Basically, if Mason got the cocktail we think he did, he was killed from the inside out. He probably got drowsy and then couldn't breathe anymore, thus the blue fingertips." Anger flashes across his face. "You want to know what's the saddest thing of all? Those dealers say deaths are their best form of advertisement. When users see a swath of overdoses and deaths, they hunt down that dealer to buy themselves a higher high."

"Sometimes it feels like the war on drugs is a losing battle. Once you try the drug, you're chained to it."

He sips at his Coke. "Thankfully, places like Tranquil Waters are jumping in and dealing with the fallout of this epidemic, trying to get people functioning again."

"But they have people falling through the cracks, too. I heard the director's own son died of an overdose."

He raises an eyebrow. "You don't say. I guess you've been looking into the place. What did you think of it?"

"Seems legit I guess, but it seems odd that at least two teens working there were using drugs."

"I agree. I'm going to check into it. Biff mentioned something about a death in their facility several years ago. Not sure if that was the director's son, but we'll see."

The waitress gives me a coffee warm-up, so I pop open a couple of creamer packets and dump them in. "What do you think about Sally Crump?"

"Just seems like a mom worried about her wayward daughter. She called this morning to tell me Ruby turned up."

This would be my chance to mention how Ruby climbed in Mom's window, but I'm not ready to share that. That would be a definite link between Mom and Ruby, which, by default, could link Mom to Mason.

Zeke's gaze sharpens. "Something going on with Ruby, besides the fact she's using, too?"

"Hopefully she's detoxing," I say. "And maybe she knows something about who Mason's dealer was. Once she's feeling better, it might be a good time to ask her."

"I'll keep tabs on her recovery. Now, I'll confess, there's something else you need to know."

"Oh?" I fight back panic.

"Someone moved Mason to your mom's yard, probably in his dying moments. His clothing shows he was dragged at some point. When you OD like that, you basically stop breathing.

This person *knew* Mason was dying, and instead of trying CPR or calling an ambulance, they loaded him up and transported him to Scots' Hollow so he would die in Pearletta Vee's yard."

Crazy hope rises in my chest. "So why would Mom go to all that trouble to frame herself? That wouldn't make sense!"

He nods. "I agree, although obviously I can't rule her out as a suspect just yet. But what that does say to me is that you need to be careful, Tess."

"What? Why?"

"Because whoever did this knew your mom's history. This was somehow personal to them. While they're probably happy your mom chose to run, which makes her look even guiltier, they might not like that her daughter is poking around, trying to figure out what really happened."

"Okay, so what are you saying?"

"I'm saying it's about time for you to go home, where you're safe. Drug dealers in particular don't care for snoops. Don't stay at the trailer park."

"I'll consider it." But not seriously. "Oh, and I was wondering if there've been any complaints to CPS about Effie Butler? She's an older woman in the trailer near Mom's."

"Is this connected to the case?"

"Not at all. I just think"—my voice wavers and I hate it—"I think she might not be taking care of her little grandson."

He stares out the window like a man of the world who's seen that scenario at least a hundred times before. But his words are backed with iron. "I'll look into that, too."

"Thank you."

Zeke pays for both of us, then walks me to my SUV. I glance around. "Where are you parked?"

He points down the street, at least a block away. "I like to walk. Clears my head."

I get situated in my driver's seat and wave as he power-strides away. Although I deliberately didn't tell him the plan I've cooked up for Rosemary, it must've been obvious I was hedging about when I'd leave. Sooner or later, I'll have to let him know someone else will be staying with me in Mom's trailer. But today is definitely not that day.

# 10

A misting rain has started falling, and I trudge up Mom's slippery, warped-wood steps. In reality, there's nothing I'd like more than to get out of this place and go home to our cozy white cottage. I can close my eyes and imagine resting my chin on Mira Brooke's dark curls. I can almost feel her soft, chubby hand in my own as I lead her up the stone pathway to Nikki Jo and Roger's. A physical ache—a sourness—resides in my stomach, and I know it won't go away until I hold my girl again.

In the meantime, I need a powerful distraction, and I know just the thing.

Zeke said someone dragged Mason's body to the trailer. Was there some significance in the side of the trailer they chose, or were they just trying to get the body out of the way? How well did this murderer know my mom?

The police have already combed the area, but it might be worth another look. They were thinking Mason had died on the spot, but if someone positioned him, maybe they left some kind of evidence, something the cops hadn't been looking for.

I pull on a ratty, hooded sweatshirt, as well as a pair of mildewed motorcycle boots I'd bought in college. Tromping out onto the porch, I throw a glance at the sky. It's a pearly gray, the kind of nondescript color that can be utterly depressing, if you let it. Since it's not full of heavy black clouds, I figure the rain will stay light.

I stride across the damp grass to the side of the trailer. The poppy heads are drooping—God's built-in defense mechanism to protect the pollen inside. It's ironic that these flowers bring such a brightness to this drab trailer, but the opiates inside them fuel the drug epidemic. Thankfully, the little internet research I'd done yesterday had disproved my theory that Mom could've created drugs from a handful of poppies.

I mentally kick myself for thinking that way. If Zeke thinks Mom wasn't involved in Mason's death, she likely wasn't.

Getting on my hands and knees, I examine the perimeter of the rectangular grassy area. Then I inch my way in to where Mason's body was, but it's been thoroughly cleared.

Dropping my face to the wet ground, I cast a level gaze across it for anything that might happen to catch my eye, but there's nothing.

I stand, trying to brush mud off the knees of my black pants. I hope Rosemary remembers to grab some jeans for me. I'm not in my element in these voluminous pants.

However, I *am* in my element with this trailer and yard. And something's not quite right.

I stand and turn in a slow circle, scanning things carefully. Pieces of the trailer's siding hang loose, banging in the wind like personal blows. No wonder Mom was looking for a new place to live, saving up money from housekeeping jobs and hoping against hope this trailer could sell.

The brown vinyl skirting at the bottom of the trailer blocks off a dirt crawl space beneath the risers. My memory sparks; I used to hide things behind a certain seam of skirting.

I walk quickly to the poppy plant, peering behind it. Sure enough, one seam juts out. I pull it back, flicking on my phone's flashlight so I can see if there's anything hidden in the crawl space.

It only takes a couple of seconds to spot a stuffed brown paper bag, shoved way out of reach. I take a deep breath, push the slippery-wet skirting aside, and slide in. I can handle the spider webs, no problem, but the tight space…not so much.

My whole body is under the trailer when I'm finally able to grab the bag with my outstretched hand. I glance toward the light coming in through the skirting's seam, then start backing out that direction. My sweatshirt has ridden up, so my stomach scrapes against the rough dirt. My hair's likely decorated with spider webs. On the bright side, at least it's dry in here.

My boot has almost touched the seam when the crack of light vanishes. Muffled, metallic thuds sound just outside.

I back up a little more, until my boot hits something solid. I kick at it, but it doesn't budge. My mouth goes dry and for the first time, I realize how stale the air is down here.

I have to get out.

I prop my flashlight on the bag so I can see the seam, but it's invisible now. Using all my thigh strength, I shove at the area where I think I crawled in, only to be met with firm resistance.

Dread sweeps over me. Something is blocking my exit. Someone knew I was in here.

I try to clear my head and think logically, but it's impossible. How dumb would it be to die under the very trailer where I grew up?

The flashlight is blinding and I reach to turn it off—then realize the flashlight is *part of my phone*. I can call for help. Simple as that.

I call Sally first, but she doesn't pick up. I would call Billy Jack, but I don't have his number and there's no official trailer park office at Scots' Hollow.

By this time, Zeke's probably heading home. It's getting toward supper time.

Suddenly, Axel's words replay in my mind. *"Call this number if ever you are overcome."*

Would he still be around, I wonder? Or is he on the road to Point Pleasant?

Maybe I can deal with this myself. Maybe there's something helpful in the brown bag. I yank it toward me, unfolding it and shining the flashlight in.

And I realize there's no way I'm calling 9-1-1.

The bag is stuffed full of Fentanyl patches.

Since this now qualifies as an "I'm overcome" situation, I scroll to the Fabled Flowers name, which is how I labeled Axel's private number in my contact list. I'm pretty sure Thomas wouldn't appreciate seeing Axel Becker's name anywhere on my phone.

Axel answers before it stops ringing, almost like he was expecting my call. Turns out he's not far away—he and his assistant finished their flower deliveries and they were picking up a pizza before driving back to Point Pleasant. He assures me he'll be on his way.

While I wait in the darkness with the trailer looming so heavily above me, I'm tempted to slap on one of those patches and knock myself out. That's completely ridiculous, of course. But I hate this feeling of being trapped.

I think about calling Thomas, but I'd only worry him half to death.

Really, this isn't an emergency situation at all. Help is on the way. I just have to wait for it.

I rest my head on my hands and turn off the flashlight, since my phone battery's nearly dead. I wish I'd memorized more Bible verses along the way. Instead, I begin to recite "The Raven," which I learned back in high school. Not exactly comforting fare, but something to keep my racing mind focused.

Finally, the sound of an approaching engine overcomes the constant patter of rain, and someone begins scraping at the skirting. Suddenly, a piece of vinyl is ripped off, filling the crawl space with the smell of rain and the dim evening light.

Axel bounces a flashlight beam around, blinding me.

I close my eyes. "Can you turn that thing off?"

"Of course."

I grab the bag and try to back up in a relatively modest fashion, but it's impossible. My sweatshirt won't stay down and I have to fit my rear through the narrow opening Axel's made. When I finally tumble onto the now-soaking grass, Axel extends a hand, pulling me into a sitting position. He doesn't seem the least bit fazed by my disheveled appearance.

I take several deep breaths and smooth my sweatshirt. Axel's assistant emerges from the side of the trailer, a large umbrella in hand. She wordlessly hands me an iced Dr. Pepper from the pizza place. I gulp it down as if I've been in the desert for weeks.

Axel reaches for the umbrella, positioning it over my head. His laid-back assistant just stands in the rain.

He shakes his head, incredulous. "It was stapled shut."

I stare. "You mean someone stapled the skirting down?"

He gestures to the vinyl piece he's ripped off, which turns out to be quite a feat since eight oversized staples run down the length of both seams.

Someone made sure I couldn't get out. I shudder to think what would've happened if I hadn't had my phone. Rosemary would've shown up eventually, but could she have heard my cries? Humans can only survive three days without water.

Axel must be thinking along the same lines. "It was

dangerous, though even without me, I know you would have survived. For instance, you brought food when you crawled below the house?" He gestures to the brown bag in my hand.

Axel's assistant, whose hair is now in a puffy black cloud, allows her gaze to travel to the dirty bag. Her level stare makes me feel like she can somehow see the shameful contents. Guilt washes over me, but I have no obligation to explain to these two.

"Thank you so much." After some slipping on the grass, I manage to stand. "I promise I won't call you again. It was just such a fluke."

"It is no bother," he says, clapping a hand on my shoulder. That single, steel-grip hand could probably drill someone into the ground.

Not for the first time, I'm very thankful Axel Becker is on my side.

The rain finally trickles to a stop as I trail them back to the van. His assistant turns to me. "Would you like pizza?"

Although it does smell delicious, I'm not going to put them out any further. "No, thanks. Thank you, again." I tend to be over-thankful when I'm nervous.

Axel gives a nod and his assistant waves. As they pull out, I have to smile. I was saved by a traveling florist. It's just too weird.

But my smile fades when I realize something even weirder: Axel didn't have a German accent tonight.

# 11

I'm still pondering Axel's mysteriously missing accent as I warm up barbeque for a sandwich. When I put it on a deli bun and add grocery-store coleslaw, the result is surprisingly tasty. My phone rings and I swallow my bite, then pick up.

"Tess? It's Sally. I see you called? I'm so sorry I didn't get back to you."

I wipe my mouth with a paper towel. "Don't worry about it. How's Ruby?"

Sally heaves a sigh. "She's gone."

"Gone?"

"She up and left. I thought she was feeling better today—she ate pretty good—and then she went to her room to lie down. When I checked on her for supper, she was gone."

I feel sick. What if Ruby gets hold of bad drugs? Obviously the heroin she used wasn't from the same batch that killed Mason, but what if he hid his fatal stash somewhere? I'm sure the cops examined his room at his parents' house, but maybe he had another hiding place.

"Did you tell the police?"

"I did, and thankfully the sheriff said he's checking into it. I can't believe she skipped out—Mason's wake is tomorrow and his funeral is the next day. I thought she wanted to be there."

"Drugs make people do stupid things." And don't I know it. "I'll look for her, too. If she shows up here, I'll call you."

"Thanks. You're just as sweet as your momma," she says.

I'm unable to come up with an appropriate reply, and my "goodbye" comes out more abruptly than I'd wish.

I finish my sandwich, dreading what I have to do next, but it's unavoidable. I can almost hear Thomas telling me it's the right thing to do, unless I want to lose all credibility.

I call Zeke and tell him about the Fentanyl.

Some sound jolts me awake in the morning, and from the amount of light pouring through the blinds, I realize I've probably slept halfway through the day. But at least I slept soundly, having unburdened myself to Zeke about the drugs. He said he'd tell the sheriff and I could drop the bag off at the police station.

The sound repeats itself—a banging on the door. I pull on a short robe from the closet and head to the door, wishing I'd had coffee first.

Rosemary stands outside, wearing a very professional pantsuit and red heels so high, it's a wonder she doesn't fall off the uneven stairs.

"Tess! Lands, girl, where were you? I've been knocking a while."

"Sleeping. Come on in."

She hefts a vivid green and pink Vera Bradley bag up onto her shoulder, then drags her glossy pink rolling suitcase into the door. She deposits both right in the middle of the living room floor.

"Guess where I've been?" she asks brightly. Her strawberry-blonde hair is twisted into a high bun, putting the focus on her peachy-pale skin.

"On the road?" I walk to the kitchen, fill a coffee filter, and get a pot brewing.

"Ha, ha." She sits at the table, pulling a lighter from her jacket. I prepare myself to ask her not to smoke inside, but she fails to produce a cigarette.

She smiles. "I've been to Tranquil Waters, baby! And guess what? I got myself a job."

I shake my head. "Rosemary, you're incredible. How'd you do it?"

She gives a casual wave. "Dad gave me a reference. And since I'd already had a background check done when I volunteered at The Haven, they just forwarded that information to Director Stevens."

The Haven is an assisted living home where Charlotte's mom, Miranda Michaels, lived until her death last year. I had my earliest run-ins with Rosemary there, and they weren't pleasant.

I can't resist asking. "How is the doctor?" Rosemary's dad, Bartholomew Cole, used to be Miranda's doctor.

"He's doing well, except pining away for Charlotte." Rosemary's nose wrinkles.

In a strange twist, my friend Charlotte started dating Bartholomew, even though he's a good bit older than her. But from all I've observed, he's just the kind of steady man my gypsy-souled friend needs. I know Charlotte misses him, too. She doesn't come right out and say so, but every email she's sent me includes his name in one context or another.

I pour Rosemary a cup of coffee and set the creamer on the table, which she eschews. Rosemary's the interesting kind of person who can look just as natural drinking coffee from a chipped mug in a run-down trailer as she'd look sipping tea at a royal wedding. I've seen her in cut-off Daisy Dukes, puffing smoke rings and four-wheeling her truck through muddy back roads, and I've seen her in an ankle-length evening gown with a tiara. The one unifying factor is her innate ability to make men drool.

I sip at my coffee. "What did you think of Director Stevens and that bunch?"

"He seems nice enough. Serious."

Translation: he probably didn't come on to her. The director goes up a notch in my mind—he's loyal to his wife.

She continues. "Lacey's really nice. And there's a dude named Kyle who's the activities coordinator or something. I'm sure I'll get to know everyone. I start work tomorrow." She flicks her lighter a few times, fixated on the flame.

"Good. I need you to watch for anything that seems off."

Thinking of the bag of Fentanyl patches, I add, "Maybe something with the drugs they give the residents."

"Got it. What are you up to?"

"There's a rogue teen I need to find."

"Good luck with that," she says grimly. "From experience, I can tell you that a teen who doesn't want to be found can come up with some really creative hiding places."

I drive into town first and drop the bag off at the police station. The sheriff is out, and I wonder if he's looking for Ruby. If so, he's probably trying to track down her car, so I'll have to take a different tack.

I mentally run down the list of public places in town. There aren't many locales where people would tend to linger during the day, except for the diner, the library, and the park. I park near the diner and casually walk by, glancing in the window for a glimpse of our purple-haired vagabond. The same men are sitting where they were last time, and a larger family's squeezed into one of the booths, but there's no sign of Ruby.

The library is next. The moment I walk in, I'm overcome by its spacious, bookish smell. All the books I devoured as a teen parade through my mind—I can visualize each cover like it's moving by on a conveyer belt. Favorites like *A Swiftly Tilting Planet* by Madeline L'Engle, *Ordeal by Innocence* by Agatha Christie, and *Hunter's Green* by Phyllis Whitney spring to mind. The only times I remember relaxing in high school were when I lounged in the library's orange plastic chairs, my mind fully engaged in story.

But Ruby hasn't chosen the same escape route. She's chosen heroin, and that means she's likely not sitting here reading. I nod at the young librarian and briefly canvass each section, but my hunch was correct—Ruby's not here.

I'm sure she could've gone to a friend's house, but what friends does she have, outside Mason? She definitely strikes me as a loner.

It's also possible she's skipped town altogether, but I still have the niggling feeling she will show up for Mason's wake or funeral. I'll go to both and keep an eye out, although I figure the sheriff will be there, too.

The park is within walking distance of Scots' Hollow. I pull in, noting they've expanded the outdoor pool I used to swim in. There's a small circle of picnic tables, each one bearing the carved graffiti and stuck-on gum teens favor when they try to leave their mark.

Since it's the only public pool for miles, the pool is already crowded. Moms stand in the kiddie swim area, monitoring babies with sagging diapers. Teens and children cavort in the clear water, but Ruby's definitely not one of them.

I sit at a picnic table, watching yellowjackets dive bomb the trash can. A guy with a straw fedora saunters my way. The fedora is a stark juxtaposition to his sliding-down jeans and Walking Dead T-shirt, which hardly begins to cover his expansive stomach.

He takes a long drag on his nearly-expired cigarette, then flicks it on the ground. I ignore him, returning my gaze to the pool.

My apathy makes no difference to him. He sits right next to me, leaning back against the table and letting his legs sprawl out.

"You're new here," he says breathily.

"Not really."

"O-kay." He smacks at a mosquito. "Nice to meet you. And you are?"

"Taken," I say, wishing my wedding band still fit.

He grins. "You're spunky. Come to the park much?"

"Used to."

He looks me up and down, then fixes me with a calculating stare.

"You look familiar."

I stand. "You wouldn't know me."

He snaps his fingers. "I know. You're staying in that trailer park. Scottish Holler."

I don't answer. He rolls right along.

"I know some people there. If you see that girl Ruby, tell her Jelly Belly's looking for her. I'm here every Tuesday."

"Jelly Belly?" My gaze strays to his oversized gut.

He gives me a slithery smile and runs a hand through his greasy hair. "That's me. I'm all sugar and no spice, honey."

Oh, mercy. Time to leave. I start walking to my SUV, half-expecting him to trail behind me, but he stays put. When I take a final glance out my rearview mirror, he's still lounging at the table, smoking a new cigarette.

There are only a handful of reasons a skeevy dude like Jelly Belly would be looking for Ruby, but I'm pretty sure all the signs point one way. He goes by a nickname, he comes here every Tuesday, and he's familiar with people at the trailer park.

He's a drug dealer.

# 12

Back at Scots' Hollow, I drive past the little boy doing somersaults in the grass. He recognizes my vehicle and stops, watching me pass by. His grandma sits on the porch, her eyes closed and her head drooping. For a minute, I'm afraid she's dead, but she snaps to as I slow and gives me a glare that would melt lead.

A real charmer.

Rosemary's truck is gone. I put the key in the door and turn it, only to realize that Rosemary must've left it unlocked. Either that, or someone's broken in.

I pull my handy-dandy gun and open the door. The trailer's quiet, but I make a quick search of it anyway. Nothing's askew besides Rosemary's wide-open suitcase on the couch, spilling over with outfits that look far from business-like.

It hits me that I never gave Rosemary a key, so she couldn't have locked the door anyway. I'll need to ask Billy Jack if he has another spare.

I yawn, still struggling to get past that first sleepless night I spent here. I need sustenance, so I shake things up and slap some hummus on pita, since it's faster than my regular tuna sandwich.

Should I report Jelly Belly to the sheriff? He's probably already aware of the dealer, and I don't have anything solid that would link him to Mason's death. But since he's looking for Ruby, maybe I should.

Deciding to err on the side of caution for Ruby's sake, I call Sheriff Biff. He picks up on the fourth ring.

"Howdy, Miss Tess. To what do I owe this pleasure?"

I explain my encounter with Jelly Belly and tell the sheriff he's looking for Ruby. Like I thought, he's well aware of the dealer, but he thanks me for the heads-up on where Jelly Belly's lurking and promises to have someone keep an eye on him.

His twangy accent softens a bit as he says, "A mighty big thanks for getting that Fentanyl to us. We're checking for prints and trying to figure out where those patches came from. I know it wasn't easy for ya."

I know he's referring to my turning evidence that might point to Mom, but it still feels like he's apologizing for the last time I had to turn her in.

Before I can respond, there's a knock on my door. I quickly say goodbye and peek out the window. I can make out Billy Jack's backward ball cap, so I open it.

He dips his head in greeting. "Just checking in. Any word from Pearletta Vee?"

"Nothing. I'll call you as soon as I hear."

He looks at me like he wants to say something, and suddenly I realize what it is.

"Oh! Rent's probably due? I can get that to you..."

He shakes his head. "No need." His gaze softens. "I'm happy to give her a little extra time. I know she's going through a rough patch."

Having a teen show up dead in your yard would definitely qualify as a 'rough patch.'

"Billy Jack, do you have an extra key? I have a friend staying over with me for a while."

When he raises his eyebrows, I rush to clarify. "A female friend. She's gotten a job near here. Just a temporary living situation. She and I can go together to cover rent this month."

He scratches at his chin stubble. "I probably have another key somewhere. I'll hunt for it. Everything holding up okay? I fixed that skirting around the side—noticed it was flapping loose."

Oh, my word. Billy Jack was the one who'd stapled my escape route shut, completely oblivious to the fact I had crawled under the trailer. No one had deliberately tried to trap me.

I had to come clean. "Um...I hate to say it, but I had to take that piece of skirting off. It's leaning up next to the trailer right now. I can get it fixed."

Emotions wrestle on his face—irritation, worry, and curiosity. Curiosity wins out. "Why'd you take it off?"

"Just looking for something in the crawl space," I say. "But I can get someone to fix it, no worries."

He works his mouth like he wants to say something, but doesn't.

I rush to smooth things over, knowing I probably look like a nightmare tenant. "I'm really sorry."

"It's your momma's place," he replies. "She just rents the space here. I try to help her with repairs, but ain't none of my business what you do to this trailer. You *are* her daughter. Anyhow, I'll fix it again this evening."

He skulks off without another word.

"Thanks!" I shout after him. As I settle back down to polish off my pita sandwich, something bothers me about our conversation. I mentally replay every word in my head—I have a kind of photographic memory for the things people say—and I realize it wasn't what he said, so much as it was the *way* he said it.

Because when Billy Jack said "Pearletta Vee," I can recall the exact inflection he used. It wasn't casual. It was personal and possessive, the way I say "Thomas."

Of course. I've been blind. For all the years Mom's lived in Scots' Hollow, Billy Jack has been around. He was one of the few people who'd taken an interest in me, often pressing packets of sour cream and chive crackers into my hand on my walk home from the bus. Every time Mom called when something went wrong with the trailer, he'd come over without delay. I always thought he was a really conscientious landlord.

But I've been blind.

Billy Jack is in love with my momma. And I wonder just how far he'd go to protect her.

After making brief calls to Thomas and Nikki Jo, who both assure me Mira Brooke is doing great, I call Sally to find out where and when the wake will be taking place. She gives me curt answers, not at all her usual Southern-sweet self.

"Did you have news on Ruby?" I ask.

"Nothing." She heaves a sigh that echoes in the phone line. "Well, it's just that Jenny Roark called me, demanding I stay away from the wake and funeral." Her voice cracks. "She thinks I'm trailer trash."

Righteous indignation bubbles up through me. "You aren't anything of the sort!"

Sally's voice is despondent. "I do have a daughter using drugs, Tess."

"That doesn't mean anything."

"I didn't tell you that Ruby's dad and I divorced her junior year of high school. Even though she held her grades together until she graduated, I feel like that sent her on a downward spiral."

"You can't blame yourself," I say. A sudden thought occurs to me. "Where does Ruby's dad live now? Have you checked with him?"

"He moved out to Oregon," she says. "I've called him and so has the sheriff, but he hasn't seen or heard from Ruby."

"Still, she could be heading that way, maybe taking a bus, if she got the money for it."

"I doubt she'd run to him. He was always too hard on her,

pressing her for good grades and kicking up a stink when she veered from his plans for her life."

"I see. Do you think you'll go to the wake tonight, despite what Jenny Roark said? Or what about the funeral tomorrow?"

"I guess I won't go to either. I don't want to add to Jenny's grief."

Sally is such a respectful woman. I can't say I'd do the same thing if I were in her shoes. I try to put her mind at ease. "Well, I'm going, and you'd better believe I'll keep a sharp eye out for Ruby."

"Thank you. Any word from your mom?"

"Nothing yet."

After I hang up, I realize I subconsciously added that *yet*. Because sooner or later, I'm betting Pearletta Vee Lilly is going to show up again. And when she does, she'll make me the heavy who has to do the law-abiding thing and report her whereabouts to the cops.

# 13

Rosemary returns around three. She explains she had to go in for employee training and launches into a blow-by-blow of her day—starting with the hot dude, of course.

"Kyle's so buff. They have a weight room there, and he must work out every free minute. He really cares about the residents, too. He said he's worked with fifteen people who've walked away clean."

I almost ask how many never walked away at all, but I bite my tongue, hoping she's gathered some kind of information about any mysterious goings-on at Tranquil Waters.

"Lacey showed me the daily routine. She mans the front desk and distributes the meds, since she's a nurse. Then this older woman named Jolene leads the meditation and the group therapy every day. Kyle's in charge of recreation therapy, and Director Stevens handles the individual therapy. The meals are catered by a food service, so I'll have to help with setting those up, as well as make the beds and things like that."

"Sorry for the grunt work," I say.

She rummages through her suitcase. "Oh, it's no bother. I did similar stuff at The Haven. Aha!" She extracts a larger plastic shopping bag. "Here are your clothes—sorry I forgot to get those out last night. Did you know that Thomas had them all packed up for me?" She winks. "Have I told you lately what a hunk he is?"

Rosemary's always been a bit enamored with my hubby. In fact, the first time we'd met Rosemary was during a date night at The Bistro, the restaurant where she waitresses. She'd flirted relentlessly with Thomas, only to be completely ignored.

A smile twists my lips as I rest in the knowledge that no matter how attractive Rosemary might be, my husband only has eyes for me.

"I'm pretty sure you have," I say drily. I pull out the clothes he's carefully folded, finally extracting a dark, cranberry colored dress and a long taupe sweater that will look suitably muted for the wake. Rosemary approves, offering me one of her necklaces to spruce it up a little.

As I get ready to go, dread roils in my stomach when I anticipate seeing Mason's body in the casket. It's a complete abomination for someone to die so young, and so senselessly.

But this death wasn't an accident. Someone with evil intent was behind it, someone who made the deliberate choice to give Mason tainted drugs and then watch as he drew his last breath.

My gut feeling tells me the killer could be at the wake or the funeral. I only pray he can be stopped before Ruby runs into him.

The parking lot at the small Methodist church is packed. Inside, the white arched ceiling lends a deceptive feeling of spaciousness, given the fact there are only about fifteen rows of pews. The shiny black casket pulls my gaze to the middle of the aisle, where Mrs. Roark leans heavily on her husband's arm. She looks like she's still in a state of shock, barely acknowledging the people who move through the line.

When I get to her side, I repeatedly press her hand, unable to think of any adequate words of comfort. Her husband drops his listless gaze to me, and I offer a sad nod. I force myself to slow as I pass the half-open coffin, which is draped with a beautiful spray of red-dipped white roses. Mason's hands are folded and barely visible, but I can make out a lingering blue tinge. My eyes trail up to his face for the first time and I immediately wish I hadn't looked. Although his lips have makeup on them, it's obvious they're still blue, as well.

In an attempt to overcome my fragile motherly emotions, I fixate on the flower wreaths and baskets I pass. A glossy-leafed magnolia wreath draws my eye and I read the tag: *Love and prayers, Sally and Ruby.*

The woman in front of me stops short, examining a purple and white arrangement. She gives a short nod and turns back to me. "We picked that one out. Forget-me-nots." Her raspy whisper is loud enough for the Roarks to hear, standing five people behind me.

"They're beautiful," I say.

"We lost our son, too," she continues, her frizzy hair floating like a cloud atop her head.

"I'm so sorry." I step forward and hope she'll follow suit, since we're blocking the line.

She does, but cranes her neck to offer one last comment. "He even went to rehab. A local place. You'd be surprised how many don't make it through the program."

That information drops like a rock into the pit of my stomach. Does she mean he died at Tranquil Waters? Am I talking to Director Stevens' wife?

She seems to get a sudden burst of speed, striding down the side aisle. I catch up to her and grab her arm, giving it an awkward pat.

"I'm so sorry," I repeat. "What was your name again?"

"Matilda Yates."

The man who was in front of her slows, and I realize she's with him. He's tall and bony, with a sandy mustache and thinning hair.

She gestures at him. "My husband, Elmer."

He shakes my hand, his long fingers giving mine a loose squeeze. "Pleased to meet you…?"

"Tess Spencer."

Some recognition flashes in his dark eyes, only to be quickly and politely extinguished. "How'd you know Mason, Mrs. Spencer?"

Now, why did he assume I was married? I'm not wearing my ring.

I give the most honest answer I can muster. "I just sort of stumbled into him one day."

"I've known him for years," he continues, as his wife wanders over to a cluster of women nearby. "Way back when he started getting his inhaler prescriptions filled. Asthma, you know."

Someone gives a light press on my shoulder and I turn. Sheriff Biff's girth fills the space behind me. His suit jacket's flared open since it's about a size too small, so the black gun in his belt holster is hardly concealed. His silky, wide tie with geometric designs is far from modern. His dark hair is slicked back with a liberal application of pomade. Although he could easily be mistaken for a mob hit man, it's endearing that he took time to dress up for the occasion.

"Elmer," he says, giving a casual nod toward the man I've concluded must be the town pharmacist.

"Good to see you, Biff," the thin man says, then moseys down the church steps.

"Lost a child himself," the sheriff says. "This town is chock-full of tragedies."

Following that pithy summation, he gives me another absent pat on the shoulder and heads toward the grieving parents.

I hightail it outside, taking a few deep breaths of fresh air to replace the stale, flower-laden scent of the church. Director Stevens steps out of a car parked on the street, walking around the front to open the car door for a petite blonde I assume is his wife. Lacey pulls in behind them, and the man who steps from her passenger door has muscles bunching under his cotton dress shirt sleeves. I suspect this is the much-hyped Kyle.

As we pass each other on the sidewalk, Lacey's the only one who stops to say hello. Her eyes are already glazed with tears, so I dig a tissue from my purse and hand it to her.

"Thanks. Just so—so hard to do this, you know? I mean, he was a great kid. Not the kind of kid who'd get messed up like this. He once told me he had dreams of becoming a pilot."

Not likely, given the stuff he'd been taking, but I stay silent.

She abruptly turns and walks toward the church without introducing the man accompanying her. The way they maintain their distance as they climb the steps, it would seem there's nothing of a personal nature going on between them.

Maybe Rosemary doesn't need to know that.

Before I pull away, I catch sight of something near the side door of the church. I roll down my window and peer at the shadowy shape—someone's crouching on the ground.

Someone with purple hair.

I jump out, leaving my SUV door open. As stealthily as possible, I run toward her, my dress fluttering up to indecent heights. But the moment she catches sight of me, she tears off. I chase after her, but give up once she starts clambering over a tall wooden fence.

Out of breath, I manage to give a half-shout. "You're not safe!"

There's no response but the pounding of her footsteps on the pavement.

I trudge back to my car, avoiding the curious stares of those who are milling around. At least one good thing came of this day: I'll be able to tell Sally her girl is still alive.

# 14

I take my time driving home, weaving around the never-ending wide curves. Every time the road opens up a little, I stare at the rounded green mountain in the distance. Doesn't matter how the roads twist, it feels like I'm always staring at that exact same mountain, even though I know that's not the case.

It's apt. No matter which way the facts point, I feel like I'm constantly running smack toward the same mountain. The mountain I was never able to escape.

My mother.

Mom knew both Mason and Ruby. She's stashed drugs under her mattress and under her trailer. She's gone missing, and Ruby's on the lam, too. For all I know, Ruby's holed up with Mom somewhere.

I pull in next to Rosemary's truck, feeling emotionally drained. What I wouldn't give for a snuggle with Mira Brooke and a hug from Thomas.

I unlock and open the door, and the appetizing scents of cooked apples and cinnamon float my way.

Was Nikki Jo's car outside? Did she sneak down here? I burst into the living room, my spirits lifting.

Rosemary leans out from the kitchen, one of Mom's aprons double-wrapped around her waist. "Oh, hey. You got back just in time for supper."

I stare.

She laughs. "Didn't think I could cook? I know, right? It's so weird, honestly. What happened is I gave up smoking and suddenly I needed comfort foods. I got my mom's hot cross bun recipe and made it so often, I memorized it. And cooked apples are easy enough."

Rosemary's adoptive mom was as Irish as the day is long. If anyone knew how to make hot cross buns, it'd be her. I take one off the plate, breathing a prayer of thanks before sinking my teeth into it.

Flavor bursts across my tongue. "This is amazing."

She smiles. "Right? I'm still kind of floored that I figured it out. How'd it go at the wake?"

"Saw some of your new peeps from Tranquil Waters, and the sheriff was there. The parents were still in shock, of course."

We load the cooked apples and buns onto plates and settle at the table. There's a hummingbird feeder directly outside the window, and we watch a couple of desperate hummers fight each other for sips of the molding water.

I make a mental note to change the sugar water. I poke at my apples, still a little disheartened that it wasn't Nikki Jo who'd made them tonight.

"You look sad," Rosemary observes.

"Well, I just went to a wake," I snap.

She gives me a surprisingly astute look with her wide-set, green-gray eyes. "You miss Mira Brooke."

I want to ask her how she'd know, having no kids of her own, but it hits me that she's right—my impertinent attitude is flowing directly from my homesickness.

Because this trailer has never been, and never will be, a home to me.

"Yeah," I admit.

"Call them. I'm sure they miss you, too. Or do you need to go see them? I can hold the fort here."

The idea sounds so intoxicating—walking away from this dismal morass and heading home. Letting the sheriff do the investigating and leaving my mom to vindicate herself, if she's so innocent. I'm reveling in the possibility when my phone rings. I slide it out of my purse and bark, "Yes?"

"Tess. It's Sally. I saw you drive by. How was the wake?"

Instead of giving a long report, I cut to the information she'll be most interested in. "Ruby was there—hiding outside. I chased her, but she got away. I'm so sorry."

"Oh, good lands. What's she up to?"

"I don't know. But I'm not going to stop trying to find her."

"Thank you. I've been calling and calling but she never picks up. I leave messages."

"That's good. She's probably listening to them. By the way, did Ruby ever mention a kid by the last name of Yates? Sound like drugs took him young, as well."

Ice clinks as she sips at a drink. "No, I don't think so. The sad thing is, it happens so often now, it's hardly front page news."

But maybe there were references to these deaths in the local paper. I can probably access it online.

"Thanks, Sally. Hang in there."

"It's all I can do."

Rosemary starts watching a particularly vapid episode of *The Bachelor*, so I say goodnight and head for the bath. As I pour some of Mom's old Skin-So-Soft bubbles into the tub, an image of Mason's lifeless young body haunts me. He was dressed up in a suit he'd probably only worn to prom.

What would motivate someone to kill a young man, just on the cusp of the rest of his life? And why? Just because he did drugs?

It *was* something all these young victims had in common—they had, at some point or another, been drug addicts. Doctor Stevens' son. The Yates' son. Mason.

Were there others? Were girls also targets, like Ruby?

I towel off and throw on the coffee cup PJs Thomas so kindly packed for me. Then I pick up my phone and search the online newspaper obituaries for the Yates and Stevens boys, with no luck. It looks like the local paper only decided to join the online generation three years ago, so I'll have to look up any obits before that at the library.

The *Law and Order* ringtone interrupts my search, and I pick up the call.

"Hey, babe." Thomas' voice does something to me, unlocks the emotions I've been trying to squelch.

Tears well up and I gulp. "Hey."

"What's up? You okay?"

I'm pretty sure God built a kind of extra-sensory perception into spouses that allows them to zero in on the words we don't even say. I try to verbalize my tumultuous feelings.

"I went to that teen's wake today. Thomas, it was... unthinkable. Not just that he was so young, but that someone stood there and watched him die."

"I'll tell you one thing—that doesn't sound like your mom. She couldn't do that."

I know that in my head. But I also know that drugs can alter behavior and make otherwise kind and good people do horrible things.

"I agree. It doesn't sound like her."

"How are you holding up? I was thinking about you today..." He digresses into the kind of serious sweet talk that would make his mom's ears turn red.

"I miss you, too. Rosemary's here now and it's not too bad. She hasn't been smoking."

"That's a drastic change for her. You still thinking you need to stay a while?"

Every part of me wishes I could say no. I want to snuggle up with Thomas and let his strength wash my worries away. I want to hang out in Nikki Jo's warm kitchen, a cup of coffee in one hand and a scrumptious dessert in the other. I want to pick up my daughter and carry her up to bed, her little legs locking around my torso and her arms wrapping around my neck.

But I feel like I can follow up on some things the sheriff might not have time for, and maybe protect Ruby in the process.

"Yeah, I need to stay." I sigh.

Once we hang up, I curl right into bed. Hopefully Rosemary will discover something at work tomorrow. And hopefully the funeral won't be the most depressing event I've ever attended.

The sound of slamming cabinet doors wakes me early. As I stand to stretch, Rosemary marches through my door without knocking.

"I can't find your coffee and I need it, Tess."

*Need* seems to be an understatement here. She looks like she has the shakes. "You should get on the patch, Rosemary. I think you're having nicotine withdrawal."

"I don't need any stinking help to quit smoking. I've been at it for a week now, and I just have to get some coffee, that's all, so don't give me any grief. I've decided I'm quitting and I will. I don't want to age before my time."

I take stock of her face and figure, still incredibly youthful in her forties. "I don't think you have to worry about that, but quitting will definitely keep you alive longer. I'll get the coffee."

After drinking several cups of coffee in the time it takes me to down one, Rosemary heads off into the bathroom for her finishing touches. When she emerges, she's pulled her cloud of hair into a messy bun, added peachy makeup that makes her skin glow, and tucked in her Tranquil Waters shirt, which fits like a glove. She gives a brief smile and wave, slamming the front door behind her. I glance out the window and catch sight of her pouncing into her truck like an attacking tigress. Whoever she's aiming to impress will doubtless become putty in her hands.

Rosemary's mercurial nature is exciting, but it gets wearying fast. I find myself missing Charlotte, my laid-back friend who has a steady personality and a heart of gold. Her comforting presence balances my driven nature. I shoot her a quick text, saying I hope she's having a blast in Rome. Knowing her, she'll read between the lines and craft a response that'll take my mind off my worries.

I return to my room, slipping into the navy sheath dress Thomas packed for me. He included a pale blue and coral scarf that doesn't really match, but I wrap that around my neck for a touch of color. He forgot my navy dress shoes, so I pull on some nude sandals and hope they're not too casual for the occasion.

As I climb into my SUV, Billy Jack walks up, backwards hat in place and a tool box in hand. He knocks lightly on my window and I roll it down.

"Hey, Tess. Stopped by to fix that skirting again. You heading out?"

"Yes, I'm going to the funeral for that teen they found here."

"Oh, sure." He absently taps his wide fingers on the car door. "Did they find out what happened?"

"Not yet. Still looking into things, I guess."

"Sally's convinced Ruby's tangled up in this. You haven't seen her, have you?"

The way he tacked that last question on strikes me as odd. Obviously any Ruby sightings I've had are Sally's business, not his. But it seems like he's doing his own search. Why?

I hedge. "Sally will be sure to hear if I see Ruby."

He smiles. "Good. See you later."

As I drive off, I keep seeing his smile. Is it trustworthy or sinister, I wonder?

# 15

Mason's funeral moves relatively quickly, since his parents are still in shock and no one stands up to add a eulogy. Even the pastor seems at a loss for words, which is disappointing. I wonder if everyone feels as helpless as I do—after all, we can't personally hunt down all the drugs and drug dealers in an attempt to save this state. Even good parents, like Sally or the Roarks, have kids who get snatched up by the jaws of addiction. How do you fight something you don't see until it's too late?

My gaze travels to the side door throughout the service, but it's firmly closed. I doubt Ruby will show up, since she knows I'll be watching for her.

We sing "In the Sweet By and By," then the pews are released from front to back so the cars can get in line for the burial. I'm going to skip the burial because I figure that's for the people who truly knew Mason well.

Someone clears his throat several times near my ear and I whip around. Mr. Yates stands in the pew behind, his fixed-on frown bringing to mind the "Man of Constant Sorrow" song from the *Oh Brother, Where Art Thou* movie. I struggle to repress my inappropriate smile. His wife stands at his side, looking equally foreboding.

He notices my attention and leans toward me, his voice a loud whisper. "It's a crying shame, all these drug deaths. And what with all our community has done to stem the tide. Why, our pharmacy has taken the lead in exposing fraudulent prescription drug use in this town."

Mrs. Yates nods, dabbing at the corners of her eyes with a tissue.

Mr. Yates' gaze narrows. "We've had people abusing the healthcare system for too long. Wouldn't you agree, Mrs. Spencer?"

This is one of those times when something that sounds innocuous is actually a very personal jab. Mr. Yates knows about my mom's drug abuse and distribution, and he's letting me know that he knows.

I resist the churlish impulse to grab him in a headlock and give him a noogie on the top of his balding head.

Instead, I give him one of my sweetest smiles. "Oh, yes, I'd agree. That's why I'm working hard to find out who killed Mason Roark."

Several people turn and gape, sending me into a spiral of shame. I just spilled my privileged intel that this wasn't your everyday overdose. Mr. Yates sniffs and turns, suddenly preoccupied with waiting to get out of his pew.

That went well.

Rosemary's always comparing me to Nancy Drew, but I guarantee Nancy would never have stuck her foot in her mouth like that. My sleuthing techniques are anything but subtle.

But Mason's murderer isn't going to get away with it, not if I have any say in the matter.

I drive down Main Street after the funeral to see if Ruby's hanging around. Having no success there, I lock my doors, then wheel down the slightly disreputable back alleys. The town's pretty dead this time of day, and the empty streets seem to mock me. Ruby probably decided it was too risky to attend the funeral.

I wish I had something to do, some way to be useful. The idea of returning to the trailer right now is just depressing. Desperate for something to keep me occupied, I call Zeke.

He's shuffling papers around as he speaks. "Tess. Sorry I didn't make the wake or funeral, but Biff said he had those covered. Anything turn up?"

"I saw Ruby outside the wake, but she ran and I couldn't catch her. So at least she's still alive. How about you—any news?"

He hesitates, and my mind races in the pounding silence. Something's happened.

"Turns out Mason's heroin was laced with Fentanyl, and it looks like it's from the same batch as the patches under your mom's trailer. There were no prints on the patches or the bag, but the numbers match up with a shipment of Fentanyl that was reported stolen from Boone Memorial Hospital."

"So are you saying my mom stole those?"

His voice is soothing. "That's not at all what I'm saying. Again, it doesn't seem likely that your mom would drag the dead boy into her yard, then leave stolen patches around to frame herself."

"True, but those patches would never have been found if I hadn't pulled on that loose piece of vinyl and looked under the trailer."

"Good point. They weren't in the open. Someone took the time to hide them, and I'm wondering why. Why drop the corpse where all can see just to frame someone, then hide the smoking gun, so to speak?" A *clunk* sounds on the other end and he groans. "Just spilled coffee on some paperwork I have to turn in today. Gotta run. Just keep your eyes open and try to figure out *why*, but don't put yourself in any danger while you do it."

My stomach growls, so I pull into Tudor's Biscuit World and hit the drive-through. I don't like their coffee, but their shaved ham and cheese biscuits are amazing and they're just the kind of comfort food I need. I scarf mine down, then reluctantly head back toward Scots' Hollow.

Going into a curve, I have to grin at the warning sign that's been convincingly spray-painted to read "85 miles per hour" versus the far more appropriate "35 miles per hour." Vandalism is nothing to laugh at, but I understand the restlessness of teens in this area. I'm only visiting, and it's starting to get to me, too.

I pull across the bridge and drive past Billy Jack's light blue trailer, which sits at the front of the park. A large air conditioning unit protrudes from one of his front windows, set at a precarious angle that gives the amusing appearance of a snaggle tooth. His wooden porch doesn't look inviting either, adorned only with white deck chairs that have faded to a sickly ivory.

Billy Jack has been married twice, and neither wife ever lifted a finger to beautify the trailer. Now that he's on his own again after his last wife left, I guess he's lost interest in keeping up appearances.

Is he hoping my mom might become his new woman? I doubt she'll bring much decorating prowess to the table, although she's definitely started making more of an effort.

It's obvious Billy Jack cares for my mom. I remember how he showed up the evening of Mason's murder, flashlight in hand.

I press the brakes. What if he wasn't innocently checking the scene of the crime that night? What if he was planting evidence against my mom?

I jump from the SUV and march to his door, giving it a series of firm raps. When he opens it, I take in his bloodshot eyes and sour breath. He's been drinking.

"You stopping in for crackers, Tess? Afraid I'm fresh out."

He's trying to butter me up, but I'll have none of it.

"Billy Jack. You know exactly why I'm here." I take a breath, then state my suspicions like they're the truth. "It was *you* who stuck that bag of Fentanyl patches under Mom's trailer. I want to know why. How'd you get them? Were you trying to frame her?"

He scrubs his face with his hand and gives a drawn-out sniff. "Shoulda known you'd figure out what happened. You always were sharp as a tack. Yeah, I hid those drugs, but it sure wasn't to frame your momma. It was to protect her."

I put my hands on my hips. "You'd better elaborate."

He steps out and plops into one of the discolored chairs. "I stopped by that night to see what the cops had done—if there was anything I needed to pick up, that kind of thing. I found that paper bag in front of the poppies."

"What? You mean the police had missed it?"

"There's no way. I figure someone dropped it off after the cops left, thinking it'd be found later and turned in."

So while I was talking with Sally that evening, the killer had arranged the bag of Fentanyl so it'd be sure to point to Mom.

I sit down in the other chair. "Go on."

He continues. "I heard you coming and panicked. I saw that vinyl flapping loose and figured I could hide the drugs there, so I pulled it open and threw the bag in, far as I could. Then later, I came back to staple it shut so no one could find it. How was I supposed to know you'd gone snooping? I wouldn't have done that if I'd known you were under the trailer."

I hold up a hand. "It's okay. I believe you. This all fits with the idea that someone's dead-set on pinning Mason's murder on Mom. Does she have any enemies…maybe drug dealers or something?"

Billy Jack straightens in his chair, obviously affronted. "Not anymore. I told you, she's plumb out of that scene. She hasn't been using since she got out of prison."

Mom's more than capable of hiding her addictions, but she's never bothered pretending for Billy Jack. If she were using again, he'd probably be one of the first to know.

He continues. "Now, sure, some folk around here recall why she went to jail in the first place. But them kids she was selling to years ago have done gone and left. They got lives of their own elsewhere, you know? Why would they want revenge?"

Good question. I shrug. "Thanks for answering my questions, Billy Jack. I feel like I'm seeing things clearer now, at least."

He humbly drops his gaze as if he's solved the entire crime. When his eyes meet mine again, they're filled with fresh seriousness. "You let me know if Pearletta Vee comes back, you hear? I keep a'wonderin' if that Ruby kid is with her. They was pretty close, you know? Ruby was all the time going to Pearletta Vee's trailer. I knew it wasn't for drugs, so I reckoned they must've been friends of sorts."

"I think so," I say. "You still can't think where Mom would've hid out?"

"You know well as I do how many blown-out, abandoned places there are around here. Wouldn't take much know-how to fix one up good enough to stay in for a while."

He has a point, but I imagine Mom would take an easier route than trying to make an abandoned shack livable, which would take some doing if she's planning on staying there all winter. But who are the elusive friends she mentioned, the ones who'd be likely to hide her?

I stand, knowing I've reached another dead end. "Oh, well. She'll turn up, sooner or later. I think."

He struggles up from his chair, nodding. "Once the cops figure out the truth, I'll bet."

Which is the whole reason I'm staying here, to hunt for the truth about Mason's death. And much as I'm thankful Billy Jack wasn't doing anything overly nefarious, he's out of the running for murderer, so it's time to retrench and look into other suspects.

Problem is, I'm tired of barking up the wrong trees. And I'm tired of mooning around for my family, but I can't stop doing it. My homesickness is a tangible thing, like a cannon ball of sadness, just pushing into my heart.

I plod back to the SUV and drive past Sally's trailer. The blond boy's playing on his porch, and I wave. As I pass his trailer, a flash of color moves in my side vision and I crane my neck to see what it was.

Granny Dearest has stepped onto the porch, and she's shouting. She's focused on the kid, apparently unaware I've stopped.

He shakes his head. What happens next seems to go in slow motion.

Granny makes a fist and raises her hand. Before I can jump from the SUV, she's walloped him in the ear. She strikes a second time, still yelling.

By the time her hand goes up for another blow, I'm standing between them, her wrist shackled firmly by my hand. Rage nearly blinds me and my entire body is shaking as I pull my phone from my pocket, where I must've stashed it before I ran to the porch. There's a small trickle of blood coming from the boy's ear, and he huddles against my leg.

Using my free hand, I call 9-1-1 and tell them to send Sheriff Biff to my mom's place. Then, without a word, I scoop the boy up, stride over to my SUV, and plop him in the passenger seat.

Granny's still yelling something about kidnapping, but I walk over and jab my finger at her face. "You mark my words. You will never lay a hand on him again." I whirl and stomp back to my driver's seat, slamming the door.

The boy has tears in his eyes, so I hand him a tissue. I press another tissue to his bleeding ear, telling him to hold it there. We pull in front of Mom's trailer, and he trails me inside without a word of explanation on my part. I motion to the couch and he sits down. I pour a glass of sweet tea, plop a few ice cubes in it, and hand it to him. He accepts and slurps it down like he's dehydrated, which is a definite possibility.

I scroll down to Sheriff Biff's number and call. "You on your way?"

"Just left the burial and I'm heading to you now. You want to tell me what's going on?"

"There's a grandma in this trailer park who's been beating on her grandson. He needs to be pulled from that place. I caught her in the act—she was pummeling his ear. I've got him here at Mom's trailer."

"Zeke mentioned something and I'd asked the DHHR to look into it, but I guess they hadn't gotten out there yet. Now they'll have to step in. Don't you worry, Miss Tess. We don't take these things lightly around here."

"I figured. Thanks."

I hang up and sit in the chair across from the tiny boy. The apathy in those Dutch blue eyes stabs me like a knife. The kid has seen it all, and he doesn't care anymore what happens to him. He's just thankful for the crumbs people throw his way.

"You're going to be okay," I say.

He sips his tea carefully, like a little gentleman. The blood seems to have stopped flowing from the cut on his ear. I probably shouldn't clean it up until the sheriff or DHHR sees it.

We sit together in silence. I'm not sure what needs to happen next, but one thing's certain—I'm not letting anyone take him back to his grandma's house.

They would have to go through me first.

# 16

A firm knock on the door makes the boy jump. I wish I knew his name.

I open it, fully expecting to see the sheriff. Instead, I nearly keel over.

Thomas. *My* Thomas, looking amazing in a white oxford shirt with thin red stripes. It's unbuttoned at the top, and his tan skin peeks out from under his white T-shirt. He wraps his arms around me, his hands possessively massaging my waist as he pulls me into his chest.

He speaks into my hair. "I cut out of work early. I have to get back tonight so I can work on a case, but I knew you weren't yourself and I wanted to see you. I would've brought Mira Brooke, but I figured it would make it harder on you to have to say goodbye again."

Tears course down my cheeks and I smush my face closer to his chest. His heart pounds in a steady, comforting rhythm.

"Hold up—what's this?" He stiffens.

I turn. The boy has crept closer, and he's standing in silence, watching us.

"It's a long story," I say. "The sheriff's on his way to take care of this little guy. His grandma beat him."

Thomas leans down. I figure the boy will run away, but instead he gives Thomas an awestruck look, like he hasn't seen many grown men in his life, and certainly not many friendly ones.

"Hey, kiddo. Nice to meet you. I'm Thomas," he says.

The boy gives a slow blink and turns away. But his voice floats back toward us, strong and sure. "I'm Brady."

I could jump for joy. He can talk. It's like my husband's man-voice unlocked something inside the boy.

Thomas quirks a smile at me and I want to give him a big, completely inappropriate smooch right on his beautiful lips. My jubilation is cut short, however, by another knock at the door.

Thomas turns and walks to open it. Sheriff Biff nods at him, as if it's nothing out of the ordinary to see a strange man in my trailer. A younger woman in pants and tennies stands next to the sheriff, smiling.

She focuses on me and speaks first. "I'm Diana, with the Boone County DHHR. The sheriff called me in to check up on things here."

The sheriff backs up so she can go in first, then he follows her. Sheriff Biff falls into easy conversation with Thomas— most law-men do, I've noticed. It's his lawyer vibe or something. Or maybe his manly-man vibe.

Diana deftly runs her slim fingers over Brady's ears, as if

she's done this many times before. Which, sadly, I'm quite sure she has.

"His name is Brady," I offer.

"We know. His last name is Shreve. He's already in the system." She shakes her head. "We'll have to take him to the hospital and photograph the wound. I'm sure the sheriff will ask you a few questions as to what you saw. Brady will be with me until I can place him."

"Place him? Where will he go?"

"We have foster families who are ready for emergency removals like this. They'll be able to take him in for now. In the meantime, I'll check to see if he has other family that might be a suitable fit for foster care while this case is brought before the judge."

I cast a wild glance at Thomas, but he's still chatting with the sheriff. I can't very well offer our home as an option without discussing it with Thomas first. Some of our church families foster and I've seen that the process is not an easy one. It would have to be a unified decision before we committed to something like that.

Returning my gaze to Brady's dejected face, I speak up. "Diana, let me give you my name and number and maybe you could keep me posted on how things go with finding a place for him?"

Her eyes soften as if she hears what I'm *really* saying, and she adds my contact information to her phone. "I will."

"Just…keep me in mind," I say, before I can stop the words.

"I understand." She sweeps her long, dark hair from her face and holds out a hand to Brady. He places one of his small hands in hers and gives me a thankful smile. I resist the urge to kiss his forehead and settle for patting his shoulder as he walks out.

Thomas stops speaking and gives Brady a wave, which is returned. I step over to the men, deliberately interrupting them.

"Let's get this show on the road." I'm far too blunt, but I don't know how long Thomas can hang around, and I need to have some one-on-one time with my husband.

Once the sheriff clears out, I dig around for one of my comfiest shirts and discover a well-worn black *Twilight* tee. It has a large picture of Jacob as a werewolf and says "One of the Pack." The minute I pull it on, Thomas bursts into laughter. It's just the kind of medicine I need on this dreary day.

"I didn't realize you were Team Jacob," he says, then gives a little howl.

"What, did you peg me for the Edward type?" I nibble at his neck.

He lifts my chin and gives me a deliberately slow kiss. When we pull apart, I take a moment to savor the golden start of stubble on his chin, the soapy-clean smell wafting up from his crisp shirt, and the ridiculously deep brown of his gaze.

I'm so smitten with my husband.

He grimaces. "Like I said, I do have to head back in time to finish something tonight, but fill me in."

I settle on the carpet in front of his chair, my signal that I would appreciate a backrub. He skillfully kneads the knots in my neck as I give him an abridged version of events. He falls into his silent lawyer mode, evaluating what I say to make connections and pinpoint discrepancies. It's only when I finish speaking that his hands still. I can't even move, satiated with my freshly refilled "love tank."

"Doesn't sound like you have a lot of leads," he says. "Ruby and your mom are out of the picture for now, and they probably know the most about Mason's covert drug dealings. The sheriff has his hands full, and I'm betting Detective Tucker does, too. What are you checking into next?"

"Well, Rosemary will be watching Director Stevens and everyone at the rehab. I'm going to dig into the other drug deaths, but those obituaries rarely say much."

"I can see if there were any lawsuits brought against Tranquil Waters, since I have access to those kinds of things. How long do you think you'll stay?"

"I've been thinking about it. I can't be away from Mira Brooke much longer—it's killing me. I'm thinking I'll head home by Saturday at the latest, so I can get ready for her birthday next week."

"It's crazy that our little June-bug is turning two already. And Saturday sounds great to me. Mom's been feeding me well—too much, actually. She's fixing enough food for two people. It's like she's subconsciously cooking for you, too."

I feel a fresh burst of love. "Tell her I said thanks so much. You want a cup of coffee or some food? I think there were a few hot cross buns left over."

He wrinkles his nose. "You've never made those before—did Rosemary?"

"They're actually really great. She's started baking, apparently."

He glances at his watch and stands. "I might take one for the road, and a cup of coffee, if you don't mind. I probably should get going. Sorry I wasn't much help figuring things out."

"It's okay. This whole thing is quite the enigma. Who would want to deliberately overdose a teen, and why pin it on my mom?"

I hit the brew button on a fresh pot of coffee and Thomas comes to my side, wrapping an arm around me. "I think it's good that you're trying to exonerate her," he says.

"Is that what I'm trying to do?"

"Looks like it from here." He kisses my forehead.

I pour his coffee and cream into a travel mug and hand it to him. "Do you think I'm on a wild goose chase? What if my mom did kill Mason?"

"Not a chance. Like I said, your mom's no killer, Tess. Trust me; I've met some serious villains in the courtroom."

I don't point out that I have, too, and one thing they often have in common is the ability to fool everyone.

I walk him out to his old Volvo. "I still wish you'd sell this thing and get a more reliable car," I say.

"And I wish my law school debt were paid off so I could do that, babe, but until then, there's no chance of a new car."

I always feel guilty that I'm not pulling my weight in the

income department, but Thomas has never once complained. In fact, he'd be perfectly happy for me to stay home with Mira Brooke and not work at all, just like his mom stayed home with her kids. I'm the one who keeps taking temp jobs to bring in a little extra pay. Sometimes I wonder if it's worth it, since Nikki Jo winds up seeing a lot of Mira Brooke's firsts, but I do sort of see them second-hand because she always describes them to me in great detail.

After a goodbye kiss, Thomas rattles down the road and I head back inside. I wander through the small trailer, feeling untethered and completely alone.

Finally, I decide I have to do something active—anything—so I gather up my dirty laundry. I'll head down to the Laundromat and maybe pick up some lunch while I'm at it. Maybe one of those elderly diner-loungers have heard some helpful gossip and I can try to wheedle it out of them.

# 17

Once I park in front of the Laundromat, I manage to scrape enough quarters from my ash tray to wash and dry at least one load. Hoisting my floral laundry bag over my shoulder, I head into the Laundromat. No one's sitting in the turquoise plastic chairs, but there's a dryer running.

I shove everything in—towels, whites, and colors—hoping I won't ruin anything if I run it on the cold cycle. Once I get the load going, I head out into the sunshine, taking a brisk walk to the diner.

The old men aren't sitting around today, but I do strike up a conversation with the young waitress. She looks to be about Ruby's age.

"Sad thing about Mason Roark," I observe.

She nods.

"Did you go to school with him?"

She chews at her big piece of pink gum. "He was a couple years behind me. I thought he kept his nose clean, y'know? But they're saying it was an overdose."

"I figure there are quite a few kids around here using."

She raises her eyebrow. "You a cop or something?"

I laugh. "Do I *look* like a cop?"

Her shoulders relax. "Nah. And yeah. Some kids come in here looking for stuff." She waves her hand in a shooing motion. "My boss won't have none of it—kicks 'em right out."

"Good for him," I say. "Did you know Ruby Crump? She might've been in your class."

"Ruby wasn't in my class, but I knew her. Had a real hard time when her dad and mom divorced. Started wearing black and stuff. Why are you asking?"

I keep it vague. "I live near her."

The waitress drifts away and I polish off my Caesar salad and breadstick. I'm running in circles. No one seems to know anything about Ruby or Mason. All I can hope is that Rosemary will stumble onto something at Tranquil Waters.

After paying, I walk back onto the blazing sidewalk. My black T-shirt seems to absorb the sun's rays and I wish I'd gotten a sweet tea to go. I shove the glass door of the Laundromat open and walk over to switch my stuff to the dryer. The least they could do is install air conditioning in this sweltery place.

One man is sitting down, his face hidden behind a magazine. I turn on the dryer and sit in a chair that puts my back to him so I don't make things awkward.

But he does that all by himself. The magazine rattles closed, and he speaks over the machines' hum. "You're the honey from the trailer park."

I give a half-turn in my seat. Sure enough, Jelly Belly's staring at me from under the brim of his fedora.

I'm not going to grace his arrogance with a reply.

"That's okay, I know I leave some women speechless," he continues. "Like Ruby. She hardly knows how to handle me, even though she looks like she could kick my can, with all those chains and spikes and junk."

I turn around fully and level a stare at him. "Have you seen her?"

"Maybe, maybe not. Why are you so interested to know, huh?"

I have two options here. I can threaten to turn Jelly Belly in, which will undoubtedly make him clam up, or I can pretend like I'm looking for the same thing Ruby is, which might get me a little closer to the person who planned Mason's death. Even though Jelly Belly might be a dealer and not just a middle man, I don't see him being clever enough to steal Fentanyl, mix it into something fatal, and inject it into a teen.

I try to look slightly desperate as I walk over and sit near him. I pull out my wallet. "Ruby said she got some good stuff from you. I need a hit."

I don't even know if it's called "a hit" of heroin, and I'm still a bit iffy as to how it's self-administered, but Jelly Belly seems to ignore all this. He gives me a quizzical look. Oh, man, I probably look too much like a concerned mom to convince him to deal to me.

But money wins the day. "How much you have?"

"Three hundred, but not here with me," I say, hoping that's a reasonable amount.

His eyes widen. "You're hard-core. I can get that amount. What are you into? Bumblebees, candy, ropies, peaches, pills?"

Are we even talking about drugs here? I'm hoping since he said *pills,* I'm on the right track.

"Straight-up heroin." I say it with a bored confidence that hopefully convinces him I've done this a hundred times before.

"Sure. Meet me back here in two days. Let's say around eight in the morning when the place opens. No one's around then."

That's the day I'd planned to return to Buckneck, so I reject his suggestion. "Make it tomorrow. And can you bring Ruby along?"

He looks confused. "Why do you want to see her? I'm already getting you the stuff."

"We have some unfinished business." I try to sound ominous.

"If you're looking for money off her, she lost her job. She told me."

So he *has* seen her since she ran off. "I don't care. Just get her to come along, but don't tell her you're meeting me."

"I'll try, but no promises." He walks over and gathers his clean laundry in silence, piling it into an orange plastic laundry basket. As he heads toward the glass door, he turns and gives me a languid once-over. "For a user, you sure do clean up well. You look like a flippin' prom queen."

"Just do what I said." The irritation in my voice is far from contrived.

He salutes me and struts outside.

I've definitely set some wheels in motion. The only question is if I can keep them moving on the right course, or if they'll wind up crushing me.

※

Back at the trailer, I take out my premade pie crust and set to work fixing a chicken pot pie. I hope Rosemary will enjoy it, but I know next to nothing about her eating preferences.

Her truck roars up around four. She blasts in the door, her messy bun a true mess now, with strands hanging out around her face.

"I thought you worked till five," I say.

"I do. But not today. Something happened and the cops came."

"An overdose?" I guess.

"Sort of, but not what you think. Lacey went out to get paper plates and cups from the outbuilding—we were planning to have a birthday party for one of the residents. I stayed inside setting up the lunch stuff."

"And?" This girl can really spin out a story.

Rosemary sits briefly on the couch, but jumps back up like she's been scalded. She can't stay still. I'm betting she was the most ADHD child ever, and this gives me even more respect for her adoptive mom.

"I went out to check on her and…she was dead, Tess. *Dead*. She was lying there, slumped over one of the boxes." She sniffs and drags her hand across her teary eyes. "What have I stepped into? What's going on over there?"

The panic is strong with this one. I try to speak in a calm voice. "Back up. How'd she die?"

"She had a needle mark on her neck and I heard one of the cops telling Director Stevens it looked similar to what happened to Mason—heroin overdose. But I know for sure Lacey didn't do drugs! She has kids and she told me she's never touched drugs; she just has a burden to help addicts."

After having met Lacey, I'm sure Rosemary's right. There's no way the bubbly, contented woman was using drugs. So that only leaves one other explanation.

Murder.

A carefully executed murder that was committed right under everyone's noses.

# 18

After consuming nearly half the pot pie, Rosemary leans back in her chair, visibly calmer. I throw out a few questions to see if she saw anything suspicious—other than Lacey's dead body in the outbuilding.

"How did Director Stevens react to Lacey's death?" I ask.

"He's the one who called the cops. He seemed—I don't know—kind of calm with it."

I'm not sure if that's strange or not. Although it seemed Lacey was close to the director—even protective of him—he *is* the military type, so he's probably trained to react calmly in chaotic situations. I wish I could come up with some reason to talk with him again, but Rosemary's probably my only hope of getting close to him.

Rosemary sits up straighter, and I can almost see a light bulb coming on. "One thing. Kyle and I were talking, and he said he suspected someone had been hooking the residents up with drugs. He figured it was Mason, but he was never able to prove it."

"You mean Mason was actually dealing drugs *in* Tranquil Waters?"

She nods.

"Did Kyle mention these suspicions to Director Stevens?"

"Yes, and to Lacey. Kyle and Lacey were actually working together, monitoring residents for signs of drug use in the facility."

"And did they see any?"

She sips a water bottle. "He said not recently, but in the weeks before Mason died, a couple of residents had positive drug screens even though they hadn't left the premises."

"Was Director Stevens covering it up?"

"Kyle wasn't sure."

This throws a new light on things. What if Director Stevens wanted to shut Mason down before he wrecked his reputation as savior of the druggies in this area?

"Maybe Lacey knew too much, bless her heart," I murmur.

Rosemary nods, then stands. "I'm bushed. I don't even know if it's safe to go in tomorrow, Tess."

Since I'm not always the best judge of what is or isn't a safe situation to walk into, I try to project a more confident air than I feel.

"Of course it's safe. It's a professional facility."

"But she was killed right outside. With a shot. You can't fight a shot—it's something you don't see coming, like a gun or a knife."

She does have a point, and I don't want her to risk her life on the off-chance she'll stumble onto some incriminating information about these deaths. The killer seems to be picking up speed.

I follow her into the living room. "You don't have to go back. We can cancel your part in this op, and you can quit tonight, if you want. It won't come as a shock to the director, since you were the one who found Lacey's body, for goodness' sakes."

"Maybe I will quit. I need to think about it. It could definitely be someone on the inside who's killing people." She pauses. "But it'll be crazy around there with them scrabbling to find someone for the front desk as well as a new nurse. I hate to leave them high and dry."

"Why don't you relax a while and then decide?"

"Good idea." She walks toward her room, then turns. "You have any nail polish remover? I brought my polish but forgot that."

"Mom probably has some under the bathroom sink."

"Thanks. I do hope I can meet your mom someday."

Easier said than done at this point.

As Rosemary disappears into the bathroom, there's a knock on the door. I open it to see Sally standing on the porch, a casserole dish in hand.

"I wanted to thank you," she says, extending the dish to me. "It's poppy seed chicken."

"But why thank me?"

"Ruby called. She said after you chased her at the wake, she realized you were probably trying to help me find her. She said she's safe."

Safe? That could mean anything. I already know she's in contact with Jelly Belly, so that can't be a *safe* safe.

"Is she coming home?" I ask.

"She said she can't yet, but she will. She told me to let the cops know she's okay, so they'll stop hunting for her."

That sounds fishy. There are other reasons she could want to call off the cops, like being tangled up in the local drug ring.

Sally smiles. Her features remind me of Ruby, and I wonder again why any girl that pretty would camouflage her beauty with overdone makeup. "I'm just going to pray her home," she says.

I return the smile. I'm praying too, but sometimes prayers need feet. Tomorrow, I'll walk into the mouth of the lion to pull Ruby out of danger, hopefully before the jaws clamp shut on us both.

Knowing I'll need backup, I call Zeke first. His voicemail picks up, so I leave a message letting him know of my meeting with Jelly Belly in the morning. Then I call Sheriff Biff. He sounds completely distracted, and I'm sure he is, dealing with Lacey's murder.

"You're doing *what?*" he asks, after I lay out my plan to him.

I repeat myself. "I'm meeting up with this drug pusher—Jelly Belly—tomorrow morning, on the pretense of buying some heroin. He's supposed to bring Ruby. I'll just need you to pick him up in the process because I don't actually have money."

"This is a crazy plan—plumb crazy. I don't have officers to spare. It's all hands on deck to get to the bottom of Lacey Crawford's death. Her daddy is the mayor, in case you didn't know, so this has to be our top priority. Besides, Sally called and said I needed to suspend the search for Ruby. She's okay. Probably won't even show up with Jelly Belly tomorrow. So I'm ordering you not to show up, either, especially if you don't even have money to complete the deal. Stay there where you're safe, Tess."

There's that word again—*safe*. But Mom's trailer is far from safe, as evidenced by Mason's dead body and the planted bag of Fentanyl.

I say something noncommittal, but someone starts talking to him and he pauses to listen. Then he gives me one last command to stay home tomorrow and says goodbye.

I walk out into the yard, trying to clear my head. That Fentanyl that was stolen from the hospital. What if I'm looking at this the wrong way? What if someone in the medical arena stole those patches—someone like Lacey? She was a nurse and would've had access. What if she said that Mason was dealing to the residents to throw suspicion off herself?

What if Lacey or one of her cronies from the local drug ring found out Mason was onto them, and they bumped him off?

Then maybe Lacey herself became a liability somehow— maybe she was drawing too much attention to their operations at Tranquil Waters.

I picture her sad face as she told me about Director Stevens' son's death. What if *she'd* been the one to kill him?

The food in my stomach curdles.

The mayor's daughter, involved in the local web of drugs. It's possible.

But, like Rosemary said, Lacey had kids. She seemed genuinely saddened by the drug deaths. And she struck me as a really honest person.

I find myself standing in front of the grandma's trailer. I must've subconsciously been thinking about little Brady. I pick up my pace, but not before the old woman hurtles out the door, screaming obscenities and accusing me of taking away her only happiness in life.

*Do not engage*, I repeat to myself. I put as much distance between us as I can. I'll take the roundabout way back to the trailer so I'll avoid passing her place again.

As I walk around Billy Jack's trailer, a thought hits me. People pay him rent, sometimes in cash. Three hundred dollars might not be a huge stretch for him, since he only has himself to look after. I'd withdraw money from our own account, but I know it's nearly empty this time of month since the bills were just paid electronically.

I knock on his door. The sound of a TV blares from inside. I ring the doorbell instead, and finally hear him coming. After he opens the door, he eyes me curiously.

I don't beat around the bush. "I'm trying to find Ruby, but I need three hundred dollars in cash to do it. Can you help me?"

To his credit, he doesn't even hesitate. "Will I get it back?" He props his elbow on the doorframe, his sleeveless T-shirt offering an uninhibited view of his underarm hair.

I pull my focus back to his face. "I don't know."

He laughs. "You're an honest one, ain't ya? But you're going to find Ruby, you say? Think that'll lead you to your momma?"

"It could."

He shuffles back into his trailer. Maybe I'm supposed to take that as my cue to leave, but since he's left the door wide open, I stay put.

After about three minutes, he returns, holding one of those navy zip-up bank bags. He presses it into my hand. "That's three hundred right there. Don't you spend it all in one place." He laughs, relieving the guilt I feel for asking him for this loan.

"I'll do my best to get it back to you." If I walk away from this heroin deal alive.

Because backup or no backup, I've decided to meet with Jelly Belly.

I feel like I owe it to Ruby. She's a lot like I was—crushed by the pain of having a dad who gave up on her. She's going to have to push past the pain, use the brains God gave her, and carve a new path for herself. But first she has to pull herself out of the abyss of addiction, and I plan to give her a serious shove in that direction.

I give Billy Jack a hug, and it's not weird at all. Looking at things in retrospect, I can see God placed him in my young life as a sort of father figure, someone I always knew I could turn to. I'm not sure what to pray for—that Mom will come back so Billy Jack can stop pining for her, or that she'll stay away so he isn't saddled with her for life.

Shoving the money pouch in my waistband, I take the long way back to my trailer. Who's to say Granny Dearest isn't out there on her porch with a shotgun, just waiting for her opportunity?

Apprehension drops on me like a heavy blanket. I wish Zeke would return my call. If he came bursting in on our drug deal, Jelly Belly would curl up like a pillbug and beg for mercy. Ruby would walk away with me and we'd all live happily ever after.

But if Zeke doesn't get back to me, I'm on my own except for my Glock. Jelly Belly didn't appear to be carrying a weapon, but goodness only knows what he could hide along that vast waistline of his.

I sidestep Rosemary's truck, then bound up the stairs and unlock the door to the trailer. Rosemary's sitting on the couch, blue foam toe spacers separating golden toenails.

She gives a nervous giggle. "I swear it's crazy, but I decided to go back to Tranquil Waters. I was thinking maybe I could ask Jolene if anyone talked about Lacey or Mason in group therapy, since that's not really privileged information, right? And maybe I'd get a chance to rummage around if I filled in at the main desk."

This is the bold Rosemary I know. Although seeing Lacey's body must've thrown her for a loop, she has rallied, and I'm more grateful than I let on.

We spend the rest of the night tossing theories around, but by midnight, we're both mentally drained and nowhere closer to figuring out the connection between the victims. Also, we don't know if the Yates' son and Director Stevens' son were killed, or if their overdoses were totally unrelated.

After asking Rosemary to poke around for details on the director's son's death, I head to my bedroom. Although I need to sleep, I can't stop spinning out various ways things can go south with this drug deal. I finally turn my phone on and read up on heroin, so I'll have more than a passing idea of what I'm talking about tomorrow.

It's horrifying to discover what nasty and potentially fatal things can show up in drugs. Why anyone would willingly choose to put that unregulated stuff into their body for a temporary high, I'll never understand.

When sleep still fails to come, I realize I haven't done the one thing I should've done first—turn this whole endeavor over to God. Sometimes, I charge into these things so determined to help someone in danger, I forget to ask my Protector to help *me*.

I also take a brief moment to apologize to my guardian angel, because he's probably stymied as to why he's always working overtime on my case. I have no real justification for my risky ventures, outside the fact that I'm wired to intervene when the people I care about are in trouble.

Miranda Michaels was like that, too. And Nikki Jo. Not to mention Charlotte, and even Rosemary. Every one of those women have been willing to rush in when others rush out. They take risks, they fight evil, and in the end, they stand strong.

That's all I can pray for—that having done all, like the Bible says, I'll stand.

# 19

My alarm buzzes too early, but I don't hit snooze, knowing I have to gear up for the morning's outing.

I head to the kitchen for a hot cup of coffee, so my brain will catch up to my body. Rosemary's sitting at the table, munching on a cinnamon bagel that's loaded with cream cheese. Her hair's a tumbled mess, but it still looks French-movie star gorgeous. I'm pretty certain most women hate her guts. Luckily, I see past her perfect good looks and into her tangled personality.

She throws me a gloomy look, no doubt because she knows what I'm up to today. I resisted the cowardly urge to ask her to follow me in her enormous truck, and instead told her if I don't text by ten, she needs to call the sheriff.

We mutter our hellos—two non-morning people trying to be civil—and return to our breakfast and coffee. I glance at the clock and realize I'd better step on it, so I say goodbye to Rosemary and return to my room.

First, I check that my baby Glock's loaded. Jelly Belly might guess I have a concealed carry purse—they're recognizable if you know what you're looking for—so I pull out the purse's detachable velcro holster and try shoving it in various parts of my jeans' waistband. It seems most secure tucked into the small of my back, so I situate the loaded gun there, strapping my belt tightly around it for good measure.

I try placing one loaded magazine in each sock, but that would be too difficult to access if it turns into a shootout. Instead, I unbutton the blingy back pockets of my jeans and slide one magazine in each. Leaving the pockets unbuttoned, I cover the entire getup with one of my mom's shirts that's so large on me, hopefully it'll pass as a trendy tunic.

I put on my motorcycle boots and walk around the room, trying to get a feel for the extra weight I'm carrying. I realize boots look way too warm this time of year, but they're my sturdiest shoes and if I have to run, they'll work far better than sandals.

Finally, I take Billy Jack's money from the pouch and slip it into the zipper pocket of my purse. I slide the purse straps up my shoulder.

Thus prepared, I walk into the living room, shouting a goodbye to Rosemary before she can critique my crazy getup. I lock the front door behind me and try to settle in my driver's seat without jolting my holster from my pants.

Taking a deep breath, I whisper one final prayer, then shove the car in drive. My determination grows with each curve I round, and by the time I ease up Main Street, I'm ready for battle. Jelly Belly has never seen the likes of a mom like me.

As usual, I've arrived early, so I sit in the SUV and watch what happens. Sure enough, someone walks up and unlocks the Laundromat doors at eight on the dot. After flipping the lights and making a brief check of the machines, the man heads back down the sidewalk, probably on his way home.

Several minutes pass, then I see a familiar fedora bobbing above a rusty Dodge Stratus several cars down. Jelly Belly pulls something from the backseat—it's his orange laundry basket—and totes it toward the Laundromat. He seems unaware of my presence, so I wait for Ruby to emerge from his car and join him.

She doesn't.

I try to peer into the car's darkened windows, but it's futile. Jelly Belly has probably lied to me about being in contact with Ruby, but I have to make certain. It's possible she planned to meet us inside.

I open the SUV door and stand, giving a long stretch in case he's watching. When I lower my hands, I casually push the holster down a bit and walk toward the building.

Inside, he is standing near a washer with his laundry basket, which actually has dirty clothes in it. I guess he's going to kill two birds with one stone: doing laundry and doing a drug deal, all in one fun trip.

I walk straight over to him. "I don't see Ruby. That was part of the deal."

He gives me a coy smile, baring a surprisingly straight set of teeth. I'm hit with a random wave of sadness. His parents probably scraped up the money for braces, only to have their son grow up to become a drug dealer who'd probably die before 35. What a waste.

"As you might recall," he says, "I said I would *try* to get her to come along, no guarantees. I asked, and she refused. Bada bing, bada boom. Didn't work out. But I do have your stash, Miss Three Hundred."

With no further ado, he slides a small Ziploc bag out from under his dirty clothes. It's half-filled with white powder. "China White," he says. "Cleanest there is."

I'm glad I took time to read up on heroin, because he just gave me an out. "Does that stuff have some extra punch, if you know what I mean? I've heard the China White does."

He leans closer, nearly bumping against me with his stomach. "You didn't say what kind you wanted. This is the best, trust me. You don't know what's in that Brown Sugar."

I channel all the anger I'm feeling because he lied to me about Ruby, hardly recognizing my own low, growly voice. "What if I like Brown Sugar, huh? That China White can be cut with Fentanyl, and I'm not stupid, Jelly Belly. Word on the street is that kid Mason died of Fentanyl. Did you give him the same stuff?"

He shrinks back. "What, are you a cop or something? I didn't give the kid nothing. I'm not the only one doing deals in this town. My China White'll get you high but it won't kill you. I use it myself."

"Yeah, well who gave the kid the bad drugs? If it wasn't you, then who?" My baby Glock, coupled with my righteous anger, give me an extra dose of aggression today.

Fear pinches his eyes and his mouth tightens. "Look, lady, I can't say, because I really don't know. There was this one dealer—Smokin' Charlie. All of a sudden, he got...smoked. I mean the dude's trailer blew while he was in it, you know what I'm saying? They said it was a gas leak but I know better, because next thing you know, I see his supplies making their rounds, showing up with buyers. So I put two and two together. Someone killed him and took over." He shifts on his feet, as if he has to go to the bathroom. "I can't for the life of me figure out who. Gotta be so high up, they got some kind of protection. Runners do their dirty work, but I haven't caught none of them yet, either."

I'm about to follow up with that astonishingly coherent line of reasoning when someone walks in. An everyday housewife with a small toddler in tow. She glances at us and I look down. Jelly Belly's already slid the heroin back under his dirty clothes.

"The deal's off," I breathe. "I won't be in touch."

I turn and stride out before he has a chance to argue. Once I get in my SUV, I lock the doors, finally turning to see if he's decided to follow me.

My relieved laughter fills the vehicle as I see Jelly Belly through the glass doors, carefully pulling his laundry out to sort it for the wash. He's shifted into civilian mode again. The guy has surprised me more than once today. Our flopped drug deal was actually incredibly informative.

Not to mention, I walked out of it alive.

I text Rosemary to let her know I'm fine, but that I didn't have any luck finding Ruby. Now I'm actually more afraid for the runaway, because what if she's sought out the other dealer—the person who's already murdered at least once, to take over Smokin' Charlie's little empire?

Who's to say the new drug honcho isn't the one taking people out with Fentanyl-laced shots of heroin? For some reason, I picture the incognito dealer in a black Grim Reaper cape, complete with scythe.

Just as I start to pull out, a camouflage Hummer whips into the space in front of me and Zeke Tucker jumps out. I back into my space and wait. He clomps over in his boots and bangs on the window I'm already rolling down.

"What were you thinking?" Somehow he manages to give the impression of shouting when he's speaking in a level tone. Must be the degree of disappointment radiating through his words.

"I had to do this," I say.

He gives me a look—*the* look—that makes criminals' insides turn to jelly. But his lips are quirked ever-so-slightly, so I give him a winsome smile.

"Do I look like I just fell off the turnip truck?" he snaps. "You're a charmer, Tess Spencer, but I'm old and that smile isn't going to disarm me. Your husband would have my hide if he knew I'd let you walk into this situation." He glances at the Laundromat, where Jelly Belly's back is to us, his fedora pulled low. "Have you gone in yet? I didn't get your voicemail till this morning—I was camping last night—and I had to book it to get here."

It's fairly common knowledge that Detective Zechariah Tucker moves through the woods as comfortably as a dolphin cutting water. Being personally familiar with the relaxing qualities of a good walk in the woods, I never question his sleeping habitat of choice. Sometimes I wonder if his wife does, though.

I answer quietly. "Yes, I've already gone in. But we really need to stop chatting here, because Jelly Belly will figure out we know each other."

"That's really not a bad thing," Zeke says. "Unless you've lined up another heroin purchase."

"I never made the first one," I say. "Now, why don't you hop in my SUV, and let's hit the diner. This stress has made me hungry, and I'll tell you everything I learned."

# 20

I share a greasy lunch with Zeke, and he tells me if I pull a stunt like that again, he's going to throw me in jail. I promise to stay safe, and he drives off to Roane County, where he's working a case. Hoping to clear my head and maybe find some information on the Stevens and Yates boys' deaths, I head to the library. Before I go inside, I pull out my Glock and its magazines and tuck them all under the back seat.

I find a cozy chintz-covered armchair and settle into it. There's a narrow window above me that affords a good view of the cloudy gray sky. I can hear pigeons cooing on the roof's ledge. The hit from the carbs at lunch and the serenity of the day forces me to close my eyes. I need to rest, just for a minute…

An irritated voice rouses me. "You need to stop chasing me around. I already told my mom I'm okay."

I stare at the girl in front of me, who is definitely Ruby, but looks nothing like the Ruby of my previous acquaintance.

She's wearing a faded jean jumper that hits her ankles and a plain white T-shirt. Sturdy granny-type tennis shoes have replaced her Doc Martens, and her hair is dark brown and crazy-curly. She has no nose ring, earrings, or makeup. In fact, she could now pass for a cult member.

"You're unrecognizable," I say in awe.

"That's kind of the point." She groans and plops onto the floor next to me. "Like I said, stop chasing me, okay? That creep Jelly Belly texted me last night and said you wanted to meet up. I told him I'd meet you if I wanted to meet you, and that he should never text me again. He's an idiot."

"He might be, but he told me there's another dealer in these parts. Have you run into him?"

She twists at a curl but doesn't meet my gaze. "Nope."

"I don't believe you."

Her green eyes flash, and in that moment she looks just like her mom. "I don't care what you believe. No one knows where I'm staying, so I'm fine."

"How are you eating? Do you have money? What about this winter, how will you have heat? Are you still using heroin?"

"Enough with the questions. I can take care of myself. Anyway, I'll head home before winter."

Thankful exuberance fills me, but I try to act chill. "What're your plans?"

"Don't know. I keep thinking about Mason. He had places he wanted to go in life, and he never got the chance. All because some freak killed him."

Uh-oh. Her voice holds a familiar, threatening edge I

recognize immediately. She's going to go after that freak.

"Ruby, you can't—"

She jumps to her feet and holds a finger to her lips as the librarian strides our way. Giving me a final, daring wink, Ruby zooms directly in front of the librarian, not slowing as she approaches a small table. She grabs her skirt and jumps, clearing the obstacle. Then she jumps a plastic chair and bolts out the door at lightning speed.

Ruby's like a Parkour jumper. Color me impressed.

I shrug at the bewildered librarian and walk out. It comforts me that Ruby has managed to concoct such a brilliant disguise—hiding in plain sight, as it were—and that she's so adept at jumping things. But that's not enough to protect her from this nameless and probably ruthless local drug lord.

I kick around telling Sally, but decide not to. Nothing's changed since Ruby called her mom—she's still claiming she's perfectly fine. Besides, it's only a hunch that she's going to hunt down her boyfriend's murderer.

There's only one way to thwart her quest—I have to find that killer first.

The rainclouds burst, swishing sheets of rain across my windshield. I have to switch the wipers on high in order to make out the turn onto the Scots' Hollow bridge. There's no sense getting out in this downpour to return Billy Jack's money, so I'll just call him and let him know I still have his three hundred dollars. I won't mention Ruby to Billy Jack, since I got the feeling she wasn't hiding out with my mom like he'd hoped.

I stuff my gun and magazines into my purse, then hold it over my head and tear up to Mom's front door. Who would've guessed I'd willingly spend so much time in this place?

I towel off and put on dry clothes, lock the doors, and crash on my bed. I'm betting Rosemary might have insinuated herself into that vacated receptionist position, thus enabling her to dig around in the files, but I can't deal with any new information at the moment. I need to sleep a bit and let my blood pressure get back to its resting level.

Mouthwatering smells emanating from the kitchen wake me. Rosemary's probably made more comfort food.

I check my phone and am shocked to realize it's nearly seven o'clock. I feel like a total heel for not cooking more. I drag myself into the hallway and walk down to the kitchen, anxious to see what's for supper.

I stop short, silently taking in Rosemary's hilarious cooking garb. She's wearing a pink off-the-shoulder ruffle blouse and pink tap shorts, making her look like some kind of glam movie star from the fifties. She's barefoot, which adds that special wild and wonderful West Virginia touch. She turns to me and I see she's touched up her red lipstick.

"You have a date?" I ask.

She quirks her eyebrows. "No, why?"

"Do you always dress this way around the house? I mean

lipstick and all?" I feel utterly shoddy with my jeans and T.

She gives a slow nod. "Yes, I guess I do. I don't really feel dressed without my lipstick."

"Hey, lipstick beats a cigarette any day. What's cooking?"

She gestures to the stove. "Mashed potatoes and pork chops. Rolls in the oven."

"Rough day?"

"Definitely. I have some new suspicions. Let's fix our plates and talk."

I'm happy to oblige. Rosemary elaborates on her day as we take turns dishing up our food.

"I managed to step into the secretary position today," she says. "Director Stevens is totally lost on that kind of stuff, and I have some computer experience, so it's easy for me. I keep his counseling schedule and things like that."

I sprinkle pepper on my potatoes and take a buttery bite. "Go on."

"I haven't figured out anything about the director—he's a tough nut to crack. But I did sit in for one of those meditation sessions with Jolene. Told her I was stressed or something, and she bought it. We did a lot of breathing and stretching, but when the people started sharing, I learned a few things."

"Such as?"

She leans in. "Get this: one of the residents hinted they could get drugs if they wanted them. Said they had a source that wasn't far away or something. I watched Jolene for a reaction, but she acted like she hadn't heard it. Afterward, I asked her if she knew what the resident meant. She said she had no idea what I was insinuating. Weird, isn't it? Then again, she *is* a little spacey."

I sip at my water. "It makes more sense for Jolene to be dealing than Director Stevens. I mean, once word gets out that his rehab is doing the opposite of rehabbing people, he won't have any more business. What's the point of undermining himself?"

"Right," Rosemary agrees.

"Regardless, I feel like stopping in to ask him a few questions. Maybe I could talk with Jolene, too."

Rosemary seems thoughtful. "One other thing. Kyle had a visitor today—a woman. I just got a glimpse of her, out by the volleyball field, where Kyle takes his lunch breaks. I was busy printing something up for the director or I would've snuck out to see who it was for sure."

I'm pretty sure this is only news because she was hoping to date Kyle. "And this is interesting because?"

"I don't know—it just felt kind of clandestine, you know? He didn't mention her when he came in, and he's usually pretty open about stuff."

"Okay, I'll keep that in mind." I sigh. "To tell you the truth, I'm planning to head back to Buckneck tomorrow night, so if you want to put in your resignation, you might as well. Of course, you're welcome to stay here at Mom's until she shows up, but I think there's no way we can figure out who this drug kingpin is on our own. I've already tried Jelly Belly, and even though he told me there's another dealer in town—a ruthless one—he doesn't know how to find him. I'll probably just touch base with Zeke and the sheriff before I leave and let them know what we've turned up thus far, which seems to be a big fat nothing."

Rosemary shrugs her elegant, bared shoulders. "Girl, whatever you think—I know you miss your daughter and your hot hubby. I'm sure my boss at The Bistro will be glad to get me back. I can clear out when you do."

Relief and regret take turns monopolizing my emotions. I'm relieved I'm able to go home, but I regret that I haven't been able to clear Mom's name, so she can return to *her* home. Not to mention, we never got to look for new houses for her.

But that doesn't mean I can't make sure she'll find a place after I leave.

I excuse myself to my room to look up nearby realty offices with an agent named Samuel. There's actually only one place listed—Adams and Belcher Realty—and sure enough, there's a Samuel Belcher who works there. They wouldn't be in at this hour, so I leave a phone message.

"Hi. This is Tess Spencer, over at Scots' Hollow. I'm calling for Samuel. Samuel, I know we met under…less-than-perfect circumstances. I'd just really appreciate it if you could show my mom houses again. Once she gets home, I mean." Shoot. I wish I could scratch this message, because it's quickly going south. "I mean I'll have her call you when she gets back from her trip, so she can set something up again. So if you don't mind keeping an eye on any places she liked, that would be great."

I hang up. Saying it was a *trip* was a stretch when she's actually hiding like a fugitive. But I can only pray this murder will be solved and she'll come back to her trailer. I find an old notebook and write a note for when she does return.

*Hi Mom,*

*I hate that you took off like that, and I still don't understand why. I'm sure you didn't kill Mason, but running only made you look guilty. Unless you're running from someone? If so, you really should let the cops know who.*

*I have to go back to Buckneck. Mira Brooke needs me and I've been gone for days. I've tried to uncover who really did it and clear your name, but I haven't been able to. Billy Jack swears you didn't do it—he's very loyal to you and in case you haven't noticed, I think he likes you.*

*Be sure to call Samuel at the realty office when you get back. I'm hoping he'll be able to show you some of those houses we never got a chance to see.*

*I love you, Mom. Take care of yourself and call me.*

*Love,*

*Tess*

I set the note on the kitchen counter. Then I pack my clothes, leaving one comfy outfit out for tomorrow. I plan to check in with Sally, Zeke, and the sheriff before I go, and I'll pay one last visit to Tranquil Waters. Still, in the end, I've failed miserably. It's time I went home and started making a little income for our family, instead of tromping around chasing after the wind in Boone County.

# 21

I sleep in longer than I should, waking to the sound of my phone ringing. When I pick up, Sally's on the other end.

"Tess, I just had the strangest conversation with Jenny Roark, and I wanted to get a second opinion on it. She called up and started apologizing that she didn't let me come to Mason's funeral, but then as she kept talking, she started cussing at me, saying she knew Ruby was a bad egg and she hoped she got what she had coming. From there, she got practically incoherent. Do you think I should tell the cops? I mean, isn't that weird?"

"Hm. She did seem pretty out of it at the funeral. You think she's doped up a bit to deal with the grief? That might make her say weird things."

"That's what I thought. But she seemed so...vindictive, you know?"

"Did you mention anything about Ruby?" My gut clenches.

"No, I didn't even tell her she was okay. I just said I was praying she'd get out of the drug scene, too. That seemed to shut her up."

"You did the right thing. Definitely let the sheriff know, just in case. But if we can't find Ruby, I doubt she will. Seems she's just venting in her heartache."

"I think so, too. You know what? I'm going to take her a rhubarb cake. It's my Aunt Jane's recipe and everyone loves it."

Sally Crump is the kind of woman who gives and gives, no matter what personal issues she's facing. She's similar to Nikki Jo. I wonder if these women know how much their thankless generosity encourages the rest of us.

"I think that's a great idea, Sally."

As I hang up, I feel another pang of regret—that I won't be able to get Ruby safely home to her momma before I go. I hope that willful, independent baby bird realizes her wings weren't as strong as she thought when she flew the nest.

I putter around, taking my time showering and dressing. I can swing by Tranquil Waters after lunch and ask a few final questions of Director Stevens, which I doubt he'll bother to answer. I've instructed Rosemary to act like she doesn't know me, which seemed to give her no end of amusement, so it's anyone's guess how she's going to behave when I show up.

Realtor Samuel calls me around ten. He sounds a bit nervous, like I was the one behind Mason's death.

"Hi, Miss Spencer. I got your message. I'm afraid I can't show your mother around next time. We have rules about showing the same clients twice."

That's a load of baloney, but I try to play along. "You don't say. That's too bad, because she would've been able to pay for a nicer home. You'd miss out on the commission."

He hesitates, then takes a different approach. "The police seemed to think she was involved in some drug activity. I'm sure you'll understand the realtors at Adams and Belcher can't enter into a transaction with a criminal."

Anger heats my face. "She's not a criminal."

"So you say. But we can't really be sure, can we, Miss Spencer?"

"It's Missus," I correct. And my "Mister" would not be happy with this guy's disrespect. Still, I can't even begin to explain things to this narrow-minded punk. "We'll be finding a different realtor. Thanks for being *so* understanding." I hang up, steaming.

Stomping over to my note for Mom, I cross off the paragraph about calling Samuel. Instead, I scrawl, "Find a new realtor and keep looking for a place." It's about all I can say.

Has Zeke looked into Samuel's background? Seems like Samuel would be one of those respected townspeople who might be higher up, the way Jelly Belly described the other drug dealer. And what if Samuel dragged Mason out of his trunk and dropped him on the ground before he knocked on Mom's door? It is in the realm of possibility. I wouldn't mind seeing stinky Samuel stuffed and cuffed.

I call Zeke to fill him in, but it goes to voicemail. I leave a longer message, informing him of my intention to head home and suggesting he look into Samuel's background. I don't add that I'm making a final stop by Tranquil Waters, because I figure I won't turn up any helpful information.

As I load my suitcase into the back of the SUV, I glance toward the trailer where Brady lived. I hope and pray that Diana has had some success finding a safe place for him to land. She hasn't updated me yet, like she promised she would. I swipe at tears, remembering how the silent boy lit up for Thomas. My spirit is moved for the small tyke and I determine to call Diana once I get back to Buckneck.

Once my vehicle's packed, I walk back in to give the trailer a final tidying-up. I pitch leftovers and things that'll spoil fast. Then I clean the bathroom. Since I don't have time to hit the Laundromat to wash the sheets, I pile them on the beds. As I dust Mom's room, I stop to stare at a small framed picture of me as a kid.

It was a school picture—third grade, I believe. We didn't have a camera back then, so school pictures and the occasional pictures taken by friends or relatives were all the visual proofs I had of my childhood.

My long hair was stringy, and I'm sure it was probably unwashed. My red shirt had a dark stain on it. My blue eyes reflected a kind of hopeless acceptance.

I brush away a rogue tear and set the frame back. Another picture—this one a close-up of Mira Brooke—sits alongside it in a carefully chosen mother-of-pearl frame. My daughter's happy, uninhibited smile and shining blue eyes speak more loudly than words. She has the love of a mommy and daddy, not to mention an extended family who'd do anything for her.

She never doubts if there'll be food on the table or a bath at night. Maybe my crazy upbringing turned me into who I am, and maybe I should be grateful for it, but right now, I just thank the good Lord He saved my daughter from the same fate.

My phone rings from the kitchen, shocking me out of my contemplation. I run in, picking up the minute I see Zeke's name on the Caller ID.

"Hey there. What's up? Did you get my message?"

"Haven't checked my phone—been busy. Something's turned up, Tess, and I knew you'd want to know."

I push the phone closer. "What is it?"

Zeke speaks slowly, like he's deliberately choosing his words. "You know I've been camping, but I didn't tell you where. It was up in the woods, about a half-hour from you. Near an abandoned mine."

I've had my fill of abandoned coal mines, given what happened to me last summer. But I urge him on, since he seems to be stalling on getting to the actual point. "Okay, why?"

"I checked into things and heard about someone who might be hiding out in the woods near there—someone who knew that area better than anyone else. It's really remote up in there."

"Is it the drug dealer, the one Jelly Belly mentioned? Or Ruby?" I ask.

"No." He hesitates, then charges on. "I'm not going to make you guess. Your dad's been living up there in an old shack, and your mom went and joined him. The men at the diner told me about your dad's place, so I went up there and camped out, just to see if Pearletta Vee ran that way."

I sit in stunned silence, unable to crank out an appropriate reply. I should've known Zeke Tucker wouldn't give up on his runaway witness so easily.

"He's a hard one to nail down, that Jimmy Lilly. Went in and out the back of the place, like he knew he was being watched."

My dad was living so close to us...for how many years?

Zeke continues. "Finally, I moved around back and had my night vision on, and I saw your dad and someone else sneaking out, bringing things in from the old springhouse. I could tell from the shape that it was your mom. I got a warrant, and sure enough, it was her."

So my mom went creeping back to Dad when things got tough. I'll give her one thing—it's the last place anyone would've thought to look, with the exception of the unrelenting Zeke Tucker. Mom never even told me she knew where Dad lived, much less that he lived so close.

"I can't believe it," I say. But sadly, I totally believe it.

Zeke seems to understand. "I just got her down to the station. I'll have to ask her some questions, and so will Biff, so she'll be here a little while. Maybe you could stop down later this afternoon? Someone'll be on duty to let you in."

"Sure." I hang up, forcing myself to accept this latest development. I'll need to sit tight to see which way things go with Mom. I'm not sure if they can slap her in jail, just because both the dead body and the toxic drug patches used for the murder happened to show up in her yard.

Doesn't matter. Things look bleak for Pearletta Vee Lilly.

# 22

I scrounge up some frozen chicken breasts in the freezer and throw them in the Crockpot with water, a packet of Ranch dressing, and some taco seasoning, then I set soft taco shells and shredded cheese out to thaw. We'll have chicken tacos tonight, something I know Mom enjoys. Who knows what she and Dad were eating in his rudimentary cabin?

I'm about to walk out the door when someone starts rapping at the same window Ruby climbed through. I'm not sure why she'd show up here, given the nature of our last encounter, but I walk over to look.

The face staring back at me gives me one of those déjà vu moments—it's like I'm seeing part of myself in someone else. The face has the same dark, Scotch-Irish eyebrows as mine, same pale skin, same slightly arched nose.

It's my dad, Jimmy "Junior" Lilly.

I hesitate to open the window, but he raps harder and shouts, "I need to talk to ya! Let me in!"

I crack the window. "Why don't you come to the front door,

like a normal person?"

He shakes his head. "Ain't doin' that. Might be seen."

"Jeepers, they're not looking for you. You aren't a witness."

"Don't matter none; we all know what the cops are 'round here."

They seem pretty upright to me, but I humor Dad and open the window. He tosses one super-skinny leg through, then clamps his bony fingers around the windowsill and hauls himself in.

He stands, dusting off his pants. He's quite a bit taller than me—six feet tall, if I recall. He glances at me, then at the floor, like he's embarrassed I've grown up.

Without thinking, I step toward him and give him one of the most awkward hugs ever. My arms hang loose around his thin torso. "Have you been eating enough?" I ask.

"Why, sure. We been eatin' plenty. Got myself a root cellar well-nigh full of canned goods—I can 'em myself, did you know that? And I grow my own garden. I'm livin' off the land, tryin' to stay ready for whatever happens in this crazy ol' world. Got water stored up, flashlights, batt'ries, all that."

Oh my word, my dad's a prepper. As in, end of the world preparations.

"I don't have any electric, either. Off-grid."

I nod, hiding my surprise. "Sounds like you've been busy. Are you working, too?"

"Retired early. Took the money and got out of the mines. Lungs couldn't take it no more."

Smoking probably didn't help, but I don't mention that. Maybe he doesn't smoke now, what do I know? I haven't seen him since I was a kid and he left us high and dry.

"Why're you here?"

He sits on Mom's couch, picking up her magenta teen spirit heart pillow and carefully fingering its lacy edges, as if it were something sacred. His legs stretch out like two ramrod-straight boards.

"You get right to the point, don't you? You remind me of my momma."

I don't want to know anything about that side of the family, so I don't comment.

He continues anyway. "She was as Scotch as they come, I'll tell ya. Didn't waste a word nor a penny. When we was sick, she doctored us herself, reading from a medical book she got out the library. She was right pretty, just like you, Tessa Brooke."

Hearing my full name coming from my absentee dad's lips seems like some kind of anathema. I make one last attempt to redirect the conversation. "You have to tell me why you're here, because I was just heading out the door."

"Sure, sure. I'll get down to it. Your momma's been staying with me a few days, and she's explained things to me." He holds up a hand, splaying his long fingers to halt me from speaking. "She ain't done a thing wrong since she's been out of prison, Tessa. She's clean as a whistle."

It sounds like he's telling the truth, but I don't know if he's an honest person to begin with. Over the years, Mom rarely mentioned him, and if she did, she was complaining that he wasn't on time with his child support.

Those delayed payments told me all I needed to know about how much he *really* cared about me.

"Okay. Thanks for letting me know. I need to run."

He jumps to his feet. "Another thing. She fell to ponderin', and she thinks she's got an idea who that dead teenager—Macon?—was a'talkin' to. Now she don't know his name, but said he was a real muscled guy Macon worked with over at that rehab place. Short light hair."

Kyle?

Dad sees the recognition on my face. "You know the one?"

"Not personally. Why didn't Mom come forward to point the cops in that direction?"

"She figured they wouldn't look past her. She's got a bit of a record with the sheriff—there's no love lost there, I'll tell ya—and she thinks someone dumped that kid in her yard on purpose. Which means someone else is gunnin' for her, you know? Likely the killer."

That was the conclusion I'd come to, but I'm not about to share. "Does she think the muscled guy—Kyle's his name—was the killer?"

"She's right sure he could've done it, but she's not sure he was in on it alone. That's what she was worrying over, and why she stayed hid all this time. She didn't think Kyle was the brains of the operation."

Dad looks at me expectantly, as if he's given me all the pieces to a puzzle only I can put together. And while Mom's suspicions make sense, I'll still have to follow up on them. I also need to tell Rosemary to watch her back today.

"Thanks for telling me this. I need to run. Hey—did a teen girl come to visit you? Her name's Ruby."

Dad shakes his head. "Nope. Didn't see hide nor hair of anyone up at my place. No one knows how to get up there, save that blasted detective who up and scared the daylights out of us. Came right up and knocked on my door, plain as plain. He wasn't messing around, neither, given the kinds of guns he had on him." Dad gives a little shudder as he stands.

I can only imagine what Zeke would've been packing, all alone in the woods.

"Okay. Thanks for stopping in—"

Dad steps over to me and grabs my arm so hard it makes me wince. "That wasn't all I had to tell you, Tessa. I wanted to tell you to be careful. If these guys are trying to set your momma up and she don't even know who they are, what're they going to do if they find out you're onto them? You're sittin' right here in the very same trailer they came round and dropped a body next to. They ain't gonna hesitate to take you out, sweetie."

I jerk my arm away. "Don't call me sweetie. I only have one dad now—my husband's dad, Roger Spencer. He's the one who walked me down the aisle, or did you even realize that?"

Dad stares at me like I just threw acid on him. In a way, I might have done just that. I don't want to encourage him by pretending he's my dad. He's never been a father to me.

I can't forget, and I'm not anywhere near the point where I'm ready to forgive, so we're at a standstill in this relationship.

"Gotta go. You can let yourself out by the window. I'll lock it behind you." I hate the imperious tone I've taken, but there's no way to temper it.

"Right...sure. I'll do that." He gives me a hangdog look. "Listen, I—"

I cut him off. "Thanks for stopping in. I'll keep what you said in mind. Bye." I grab my purse and sling it over my shoulder, staring at him until he opens the window. He gives me a final, bewildered look, then scoots out. The moment I hear his feet hit the ground, I lock the window and stride out the front door.

A car's engine revs several times, then Dad finally clatters out from behind the house. He's driving a rusty red Volkswagen bug that has been cobbled together with a bright blue door and painted white bumpers, giving it a haphazard patriotic look.

He tosses me a half-hearted wave and hits the gas, which gives the car a tiny puff of speed.

I lock the front door behind me. If Mom comes home, I'm sure she can bum a key from Billy Jack, who'll be more than happy to welcome her.

I shoot a quick text to Rosemary, warning her not to be alone with Kyle and letting her know I'll be over soon. I drive out slowly, hoping I don't get behind my dad, because I really don't want to see him again.

It doesn't matter how much I lie to myself and to him; Junior Lilly is still my biological dad. His blood runs in my veins. I'll never outrun that fact.

As I pull onto the road, green leaves flutter overhead, shading my car from the hot sun like a protective umbrella. The familiar, shady drive pushes me right back into my teen years, when I used to imagine blissful reunion scenes with my dad. I was sure he'd pull me into a bear hug, much like Roger does now, and tell me how proud I made him and how much he loved me.

But even then, I knew the reality would be a disappointment, as it had been today. Dad had barely reciprocated my impulsive hug.

Ruby's in the same boat—longing for a relationship with her dad, but knowing it'll never live up to the Disney version of things.

Some Cinderella stories are even scarier than the original, because it's your own flesh and bone who've turned against you, not some crazy stepmother.

But just like in Cinderella, there is always that tiny ray of hope. I pray Ruby finds her own ray and follows it out of the shadowy forest she's gotten stuck in.

# 23

Tranquil Waters looks relatively dead today, with only a handful of cars parked outside. True to form, Rosemary's parked her huge truck right on the painted white line, so it takes up two spaces. I pull in right next to it, as close as I can get, deliberately blocking her driver's door. She probably won't see it before I leave, but it gives me a good, long laugh as I pull my purse from the car.

My uninhibited laughter draws the attention of a woman sitting in the passenger side of a nearby car. I can't quite make out her face, but she's suddenly leaned forward, so I know she's watching me. I clear my throat, as if the random laughter is some kind of tic.

I walk toward the French doors. Once inside, the cool of the air-conditioning washes over me like a fresh breeze. There's a new flower display on the center table, this one even more striking than Axel's last, so I'm sure he's arranged it. Grassy-looking leaves swirl around purple orchids in a water-filled, enclosed glass vase. It has a slightly hypnotic effect as you gaze into it.

"Hello, ma'am, may I help you?"

Rosemary has affected a slightly nasal tone and I have to fight to maintain my composure as I walk over to the front desk. "Yes, you could. My name is Tess Spencer—Mrs. Spencer—and I would like to talk with Director Stevens."

"Let me check his schedule." She taps a few keys, then stares blankly at her oversized computer screen. "Yes, he could see you now."

She shoots me a conspiratorial wink, then comes out to greet me. As we walk down the long hallway, she whispers, "The pharmacist is in there with him, but he was just making a drop off and I figure he's leaving soon."

The pharmacist—Mr. Yates? It hits me that it could've been Matilda Yates sitting in that car, watching my fit of laughter. It's interesting that she accompanies her husband on his deliveries.

We're nearing the director's office when I ask, "Did you get my text?"

She nods, arching a blonde-ginger eyebrow. "I'm watching my back. You'll have to explain later. But Kyle hasn't even come in today, anyway."

Mr. Yates says a loud *goodbye*, then charges past us, hardly glancing my way. Too bad—he missed a prime opportunity to lecture me on abuse of prescription meds, adding to my load of misplaced guilt for my mom's crimes of the past.

Rosemary pipes up, trying to be bubbly, but she sounds more like a squeaky Betty Boop. "Someone to see you, Director!"

Director Stevens stands and meets me at the door, taking my hand in his sturdy grip and giving it a firm shake. "Thank you, Rosemary."

There are no inflections of attraction in his tone, no underlying flirtation, and again, I'm impressed with his loyalty to his wife.

He motions to the chair and returns to his own seat. "Mrs. Spencer. Are you here in your detective capacity this time? What brings you back to Tranquil Waters?"

I've decided to be really up-front with Director Stevens, because I think that's something he'd appreciate.

"I'm not actually a detective. Just looking into things, like I said. Mostly for Mrs. Crump."

He rubs his square chin. "Sure."

He sounds like he doesn't believe me one bit. I wonder if he's talked to Sally Crump, and if so, what she's told him about Ruby.

I plunge on. "I have some difficult questions to ask, so I can help Mrs. Crump find her daughter. I'm going to throw them out there, point-blank, and if you don't want to answer, just kick me out."

His eyes widen. "You're a bold woman, Mrs. Spencer. I respect your honesty. I'll try to help."

"First, did you realize someone was, and possibly still *is,* slipping drugs in to your residents?"

He doesn't even feign shock. "I knew about Mason. But you're telling me someone else is dealing in my facility?"

"Yes. Don't you give your residents periodic drug tests to catch this kind of thing?"

"I do, but there's also a turnover rate like you wouldn't believe. People enter the program, then they leave before they've even gotten started. While that's typical across the board, I'll confess our in-and-out rate is pretty high. That could account for it." He leans in, arm muscles rippling in an impressive fashion for an older man. "Do you have someone specific I need to be watching?"

"I do, but I need a little more information first. I know this is extremely callous, and I wouldn't ask if I didn't think it would help lead me to Ruby. Lacey had told me a little about your son's death. When did that happen, and could you share some details about it? I haven't been able to turn up anything."

He looks toward his window, avoiding my eyes as he speaks. "My son, Chris, died of an overdose of OxyContin eight years ago. Then his friend, Henry Yates, died not long afterward, of the same type of overdose. I mourned for too long, but my wife finally gave me the kick in the pants I needed. She encouraged me to partner with my dad, who had just opened Tranquil Waters. Eventually, I took over." He groans. "But with Mason's death and Ruby's disappearance, not to mention your allegations there's a dealer operating right under my nose, I feel like I'm shadow boxing, not making any real difference."

I sit quietly, processing this new information. So the Yates boy and the Stevens boy were friends, and they died the same year. And that was eight years ago…no wonder I hadn't been able to find their obituaries. Eight years ago, I was in college, and my mom was dealing Oxy. Did she deal both teens straight to their deaths?

I try to meet the director's despondent gaze, feeling utterly conflicted myself. "I know you're making a difference. I've heard that many people have left Tranquil Waters completely rehabbed. You can't blame yourself for these accidents."

He looks like he doesn't believe my reassurances, any more than I believe my mom had nothing to do with those deaths eight years ago.

If Mom's drug-dealing was the suspected cause of those deaths, it makes sense that someone in either the Yates or the Stevens family would be very interested in setting her up for a fall the moment she got out of prison.

I'm ruling out Director Stevens, because he joined this rehab place almost as a penance, to help others who were struggling like his own son. I don't think he'd want to take out another teen just to stick it to Mom.

I remember what Jelly Belly said about someone in a high position in town. The mayor is the highest position, and Lacey's dad is the mayor.

"What can you tell me about Lacey?" I ask.

Fresh regret floods his features. "She was like an angel to these residents. She had the patience of Job dealing with the mood swings drug users struggle with."

"Did she and Kyle tell you they suspected Mason was dealing in the facility?"

"They did. We all agreed to keep an eye on him, but not long after that, his body was found."

He politely doesn't mention *where* Mason was found.

I give a desperate poke in the dark. "Did Lacey's dad ever stop in here?"

"The Mayor? He came for the opening ceremony, but that was about it. Why?"

"Just trying to get a feel for his character, I guess." Also, it's rude to come out and ask if he's a drug dealer.

Another idea hits me. "Do you have video surveillance on this place?"

He nods. "We do. One outdoor and one indoor camera. But the police already checked the footage and found nothing from the day Lacey died. The outdoor camera is aimed left, toward the driveway and ball field, so the outbuilding isn't in the picture. The camera catches a little bit of the parking lot, but there were no unusual cars in sight. The cops said the killer probably parked off-site and walked through the woods to the outbuilding."

I might not be able to get anything new from the video the day Lacey died, but what about yesterday, when Kyle was talking to a woman on the volleyball court? Maybe it'll show me her face.

"Actually, I was wondering if I could look at the footage from yesterday?"

"I can pull that up for you. But why?"

"I'm not sure. Just a hunch."

He starts jamming at his computer keys, uttering a few choice words each time the process seems to slow. He pulls a scrawled-on sheet of paper from his drawer—presumably passwords—before typing a bit more. Finally, he turns the screen toward me. It's a split-screen with two black-and-white feeds.

He stretches his tattooed arms in front of him and yawns. "I need to take a lunch break, but you go ahead and look over those. Might take a while, though. If you get hungry, just go down to the cafeteria and tell them I said you get a free lunch."

I smile as he makes his way past me. "Thanks so much."

# 24

I don't want to waste time in case Kyle comes sniffing around, so I pick the outside feed and hit play at the 11:30 mark, since Rosemary had said Kyle met the woman on his lunch break.

There's no one to be seen, just a few cars coming and going, until 12:41. Then I can see the back of a man who's walking across the grass. He has light hair like Kyle, and it's definitely his build. He's carrying a brown lunch bag and he strides to the far end of the volleyball court.

Then he stops. He doesn't sit to eat, he just stands.

I watch for five minutes...ten...and the silent film rolls on, with nothing happening. He's still standing, gripping the brown bag.

A brown bag like the one someone planted on my mom?

Finally, I see movement at the edge of the woods, and a woman steps out, walking quickly toward Kyle.

She has short dark hair, a long dress, and surprisingly white tennis shoes.

I zoom in on her face, confirming my fears. It was Ruby.

She must've been meeting Kyle for drugs. Is *he* the dealer?

I continue to watch as she starts talking to him. I expect him to hand over the bag, but he doesn't.

He does something that's far worse.

He snakes an arm around her waist, yanks her toward him, and...

He kisses her. Full on the lips. His hands roam to places they shouldn't. The mommy in me wants to reach into that screen and kick his hiney.

They finally tear themselves apart, and Ruby disappears into the woods. Kyle turns, and I don't have to zoom in to make out his satisfied smirk. He pulls out his lunch, munching on it as he walks back toward the main building.

So Ruby was the mystery woman, and she's with Kyle. Does that mean she was leading Mason on? Could *Ruby* be the one who gave Mason a fatal dose of mixed heroin? Maybe Mrs. Roark was right and Ruby was the bad egg.

There's no way I can believe that. Every time I see Ruby, all I see is a teen who wants to escape who she is. Not a killer.

Rosemary sweeps in, casting nervous glances behind her. "Did you find out anything?"

"I did. Turns out Kyle's dating Ruby. I don't know how long it's been going on, and I don't know if they had anything to do with Mason's death. I'm pretty sure Director Stevens wasn't involved, though."

"Girl, I'll tell you what. Kyle's still not here. You think he left town, maybe with Ruby?"

I pound my fist into my hand. "Could be. I hate that she's with him—he's so much older than her."

"The heart wants what it wants," she quips.

"Is that supposed to be pithy?"

She frowns. "I've dated more than you, so I know more about these things."

"So now you're an expert on love?"

Rosemary opens her mouth to retort, but the director walks in, carrying a cup of coffee. His gaze travels from me to Rosemary, then back to me. "You two know each other?"

Rats, he probably overheard some of our weird conversation.

"A little. I've seen her around some." I turn the computer screen back toward his desk and Rosemary whirls out into the hallway, leaving me to fend for myself.

Director Stevens situates himself behind the desk once again. I figure he could scold me for watching the footage in front of a brand new employee, but he doesn't.

Instead, he takes a long sip of coffee, then asks, "Find anything?"

"Kyle met up with Ruby Crump on the volleyball court yesterday." I walk around and pull up the video segment so he can watch it.

His brow furrows as he sees the exchange on the monitor. He finally lifts his concerned gaze toward mine. "Should we tell the police?"

"I don't know, since it's pretty obvious their meeting was of a romantic nature. Would you mind calling Sally Crump and telling her those two are involved? In the meantime, if it's okay, I'd like to look around that outbuilding. I know the police have already been over it, but maybe Lacey left some kind of clue as to her attacker, and they didn't know what they were looking for."

He looks dubious, but he pulls a key ring from a lower drawer and points out the key to the outbuilding. He drops the key ring in my open hand.

Picking up his mug and swirling the coffee around, he asks, "What should I do if Kyle shows up for work?"

"Just act normal," I say. "Even if we suspect he's the one dealing drugs in your rehab, we have no proof. Just watch him closely."

"I will." His jaw clenches and his knuckles turn white as he grips his mug. It's not going to be pretty if he catches Kyle with drugs.

I smile. "Thank you for being so helpful. I have to confess that I'm not sure *why* you're helping me, but I appreciate it."

Steam rises from his mug and he gives a half-grin, which considerably softens the angles of his face. "Because you remind me of my wife. She's as pigheaded as they come, and without her, I would've given up. Y'all are the ones who shake things up for the better."

I pocket the key ring as I walk out, smiling from ear to ear.

Rosemary's not behind the desk as I walk out, so I scrawl a quick, cryptic note to let her know my mom's showed up.

*Thanks for your help today. Thanks for asking about my mom—she'll be home tonight.*

*-T*

I make a mental note to apologize for our argument. Rosemary's still learning about love, even though she'd never admit it. Goodness knows she's regaled Charlotte and me with enough horrid dating tales to illustrate that the heart often doesn't have any idea what it wants.

The sky is a shocking, brilliant blue, and the sun's force seems to have doubled. I wish I'd worn shorts or a sleeveless shirt, but in lieu of that, I roll up the ankles of my jeans and sleeves. I'm betting that outbuilding will be scalding hot.

The outbuilding is a long, metal structure backed up against the tree line. I walk up a couple of cinderblock steps and insert the key in the padlock. After propping open the metal door, I find a light switch on the side wall and hit it, only to find there's no light bulb screwed into the socket. Since there are no windows, the open door provides the only light, and that's not enough to make out things in the back of the building.

I carry a small flashlight in my purse, so I unzip the middle pocket and feel around for it. My hand closes over the flashlight just as a bee stings my upper arm. I slap at the pain, then spin around, swatting at the air to make sure the bee's gone.

The bulky shadow of a man stands right behind me. I shove

him away, but his dark, muscular form seems to shift and blur.

"Kyle," I say, but my words blur, too.

"Nighty-night." He steps aside and watches as I drop to the ground.

# 25

It's dark when I wake up. Is it night, or am I inside a dark room?

I try not to panic, counting my blessings that I woke up at all, unlike Mason or Lacey. Did someone have mercy on me, or did they keep me alive so I could experience an even worse death?

My mind is still fuzzy and my vision bleary, but as my eyes adjust to the darkness, I slowly take stock of my surroundings. I'm lying on a twin bed in a medium-sized room. There's a beanbag in the corner near a TV and legs extending to bare feet protrude from it.

I scoot back on the bed, hoping Kyle isn't sitting over there, waiting for me to wake up.

I stare harder on the beanbag, wishing I had night vision. It looks like there's no torso to accompany the legs.

I stifle a gag. Surely this isn't some sadistic gang of murderers...

I have to see what's going on, to get prepared for whatever lies ahead. I force my muscles to move in tandem, managing to roll off the side of the bed. I try to soften the thud as my body hits the floor, but I don't succeed. If we're on an upper floor, which it sounds like, whoever is downstairs will have heard me.

I drag my uncooperative body toward the legs. The feet are small and probably belong to a female, so that gives me hope. If this person is alive, it's not Kyle.

I'm almost to the point where I can see the torso and head, if they are still connected, when the feet move.

I scuttle backward. Adrenaline floods my body, making it fully functional again.

A head rises from its resting place on the opposite side of the beanbag. A garbled voice mutters something that I can't make out, then repeats it.

"Can't…trust men."

The voice is familiar. I replay it in my mind, trying to place it. When I do, I realize I don't just have my own life to worry about.

"Ruby?" I ask.

She leans forward, her body flopping toward me. "You. Why're you here?"

"The better question is what are *you* doing here? Did he drug you, too?"

Her voice becomes clearer. "Guess so. Kyle told me to meet him at this old house. Minute I walked in, something jabbed my arm."

My suspicions are confirmed. "I take it this isn't Kyle's house, so where are we?"

"Last house on some back street. I forget the street name or the name on the mailbox."

"Think *hard*, Ruby. What did you notice about the house? Were there people living nearby we could shout out the windows to? What does the house look like?"

She ponders for what seems like forever. I nudge her foot, afraid she's drifting to sleep.

"Hey, cut it out. I was picturing the place. The houses next to it didn't seem to have people around. This is a tall house, like three stories? Some gables, that kind of thing. Shutters falling off and stuff, but not abandoned."

I wobbily stand to my feet and try to get a feel for the room. There's a light switch that doesn't work—just like in the outbuilding. Kyle wants us to stay in the dark, in more than one way. I can't make out a window anywhere, but maybe they blacked it out somehow.

I whisper. "Why would Kyle knock you out? It looked like you two were an item."

"Yeah, about that. I put two and two together and realized that since Kyle was the only one from Tranquil Waters who ever visited Mason's place, he must've been his dealer. I hit on Kyle and told him I was in withdrawal—which I'm not, Tess—and he seemed to buy it. He said he'd score me more heroin. In the meantime, he seemed to be falling for me and I fed him some line about wanting to run away and live in Arizona with him."

"Turning on the old feminine charm. That was totally risky, Ruby."

"Obviously," she retorts.

I find the door and turn the knob, but it's firmly locked. "He must've figured out you were trying to get close so you could turn him in. And he knew I was at Tranquil Waters, checking into things. So he gave us some kind of knockout drugs and locked us in here. Now what's he going to do?"

Ruby struggles to her feet. "There's no window in here. We can't get out."

I try to breathe calm into this situation, despite my own racing pulse. "There's always a way out. In this case, it's the way in. He's not expecting us to be mobile, because he didn't bother to bind our hands or feet. I'm betting he didn't know how long the drugs would last and he miscalculated."

"How did he get the drugs? You think he's a dealer?"

It doesn't fit the description Jelly Belly gave me, but then again, he wasn't sure who the new dealer was. Maybe Kyle's better connected than I thought. Does the mayor protect him? Or is the sheriff involved? Maybe Sheriff Biff makes a show of pulling in smaller distributors, like my mom, but leaves the big fish alone?

Try as I might, I can't see Kyle as a big fish. He might've killed Mason and Lacey to silence them, but why set up my mom? He's too young to know about her history.

Which brings me back to someone older as the kingpin—someone like the sheriff or the mayor.

"So what do we do now?"

Ruby's voice is filled with the despair I'm trying not to feel.

If Kyle didn't bother to hide my things, it's possible the director or Rosemary might notice my abandoned purse in the outbuilding or my SUV outside. But by then, it might be too late.

"I say we find weapons and the moment Kyle steps in, we attack him." Not for the first time, I determine to buy a belt holster for my Glock so it'll be on my person at all times. Of course, it probably would've been noticed and confiscated when Kyle moved me here, but what if it hadn't? We would've really had the upper hand.

I shove those thoughts from my mind. "Feel for sharp or heavy objects. We want to incapacitate him if we can."

For the next few minutes, we busy ourselves gathering things. It becomes obvious that this is a boy's room. Ruby finds a stash of Legos that she sprinkles in front of the door. She also finds a heavy toy tractor and a skateboard.

I take a few video game discs and break them in half. I'm thinking the sharp edges could slash like small blades. I've just picked up a can of body spray when the door creaks open, letting in some light from the hallway outside.

Kyle strides in, then stumbles on the blocks. "Ow! What the—"

"Now!" I shout, releasing an aerosol cloud into the room as I spray his eyes.

Ruby whaps him in the head with the skateboard, and he lunges for her. I stab his arm with a disc and plunge another into his neck, while Ruby takes a wild swing with the tractor.

It catches my arm instead, and I trip backward.

"Get out!" I tell her, rubbing my sore arm. "Get help!"

Kyle gains his footing and menaces my way as Ruby races out the door. She hesitates in the hallway. "We're in the attic!" she shouts.

I hear her stumbling down the stairs as I unleash the spray again. This time, it peters out. Kyle moves closer and I grip the round edge of the disc, slashing at his arms.

Ruby's desperation-filled voice drifts up to us. "It's locked!"

"Find another way!" I scream.

It takes a moment, but then I hear a heavy window sliding open. At the same time, Kyle's arms imprison me like a steel trap.

"I'm going out!" Ruby yells.

I hate to fathom what that means since we're on the attic floor. I pray Ruby doesn't jump to her own doom.

Kyle grabs my arms, making me wince. "You witch! Stop wiggling around!"

He's a lot taller than I am, otherwise I might try one of those headbutting moves I've seen in movies. I'd probably only crash into his muscled chest and knock myself out.

So I do the next best thing. I summon all my strength and thrust my knee into his groin.

He screeches and lets go for one glorious moment. I tear out of the room, slamming the door behind me. Knowing I probably can't make the jump Ruby had to make, I veer toward the steps. I figure if I gain enough momentum going down, I can crash into the door and force it open.

When I hit the second stair from the bottom, I jump and throw my body into the old wooden door. Much to my surprise, it gives and bursts open, depositing me in a heap on the floor.

I fumble to my feet, glancing up as I do so.

"You might as well sit down," a calm voice says.

I stare at the source of the voice. A woman sits on a couch directly facing me, her frizzy hair backlit by a window. She's holding a large revolver.

She leans toward me. "Hello, Tess. You would've saved yourself a bushel of trouble if you'd just given up on your mom a long time ago, like we did."

# 26

Matilda Yates yawns like a cat, keeping the gun aimed at me.

Stunned speechless, I can't even force myself to move out of her line of fire.

She talks to me like we're chatting over dinner. "Are Kyle and Ruby coming down soon? That was quite the ruckus up there."

Her smile is genuine, not the least bit unhinged. I try to run escape scenarios through my mind, but with a gun in front of me and the door right next to Matilda, there's just nothing that will work.

"Are we at your house?" I ask stupidly.

Footsteps clunk behind me as Kyle makes his way down the stairs. He shoves my shoulder, pushing me out of his way. He glares at me with eyes reddened by the body spray.

Matilda answers, as if oblivious to Kyle's manhandling. "Yes. You were actually in my Henry's room. I've kept it exactly the same, all these years."

Kyle stomps over to her side, extending a scratched hand. "Give me the gun," he demands.

"Oh, no, I don't think so. That's not how we were going to kill her. Where's the girl?"

Kyle grunts. "Jumped out the window."

"Upstairs? Oh, dearie me. That was really dangerous."

I pipe up. "Um, Mrs. Yates? In case you haven't noticed, this entire situation is really dangerous. Now, I think you'd better let me walk out of here, or you know the sheriff will lock you up."

Matilda motions to Kyle. "You go on downstairs and keep watch. I need to talk with Mrs. Lilly—I mean Mrs. Spencer—for just a minute."

Kyle's puffy eyes swing back to me. It's obvious that he'd like to strangle me right here. He seems to fight his instinct and stalks out the door instead, so I'm betting he's handsomely paid.

Matilda's bright gaze returns to me. "Now then, I'm sure you have some questions. I want to tell you a few things before…the end…because I think you deserve to know what really happened. Have a seat."

Unable to fathom an alternate course of action, I sit in a chair near her.

She settles back against the couch cushion, but the gun remains firmly in-hand. "My Henry left me eight years ago this fall. He was so full of potential, but he fell in with the wrong friends—like Mick Stevens' boy—and next thing we knew, he was stealing money for drugs."

I wish she'd get to the point, but then again, I don't.

"As soon as Chris Stevens died of his overdose, we checked Henry in to Tranquil Waters. I'm sure Mick Stevens wished he'd put his son in there, but he was probably in denial that his kid had become a user, just like all the addicts he worked with."

I nod.

Her voice is getting increasingly scratchy, and she licks her dry lips. "So once Henry was in the program, we figured he would be safe. But someone got to him, gave him more OxyContin, and he quit the program. Took me all these years to figure out who it was. I'll bet you can't guess?"

She shoots me a sickly-sweet smile.

And I know.

"Your momma," she continues. "Yes, Pearletta Vee certainly had her fingers in a lot of pies back then, making money off the demise of our youth. There weren't any big-time dealers around then, not like I am."

My eyes widen, and I'm sure she reads the shock on my face.

She keeps talking, glossing over the bomb she just dropped. "She was really clever—so clever, my husband didn't even suspect, and he was the one filling her prescriptions! But she must've had another supplier to get her hands on all those pills. Then, just a couple years ago, I talked to Mick and he let it slip that Pearletta Vee had worked at Tranquil Waters for a brief time. He'd let her go because she was erratic keeping her work hours. So I had Lacey look into things for me—that girl was always so helpful—and she found a few paystubs for your mom. I knew then that Pearletta Vee had done it—she'd killed my

Henry. It was too bad that after Mason's funeral, Lacey remembered that favor she'd done me and she started asking questions, so I had to silence her."

I don't want to hear the rest, but she's rolling toward her grand finale.

"By the time I'd put two and two together, Pearletta Vee was in prison and I couldn't get to her. So I started laying the groundwork for my revenge. I took over Smokin' Charlie's ring—he was so obvious—and I got Jelly Belly to help me distribute. I paid him to tell you a pack of lies and act like he was a dealer. In reality, he works for me, just like Kyle and everyone else in this town."

She's so smug. But it doesn't make sense. I lean forward. "Why would you turn into a dealer, just like my mom? You were the one putting them on the wrong path!"

Matilda adjusts her embroidered denim vest. "I always think long-term, dear. It was easy enough to get kids hooked. Then, when your mom was released, I had a plan to pin overdose deaths on her. After all, what's another druggie's death? They're eventually going to kill themselves, anyway. I just sped things along for Mason, and I was going to help Ruby out, as well." She clicks her tongue in derision. "Did you know that Ruby had asked Kyle for more heroin? Poor child. I decided to put her out of her misery. And when Jelly Belly told me *you* were looking for heroin, why, I could hardly believe it! Not only could I frame Pearletta Vee, I could frame her for *her own daughter*'s death!"

She gives a sigh of satisfaction, as if she's just painted a masterpiece. "So that brings you right up to speed. I knew you'd want to know the truth about your mother before you died. Obviously, she's done a poor job parenting, for you to be seeking heroin while you're in town."

I don't even bother to contradict her.

She stands, her frowsy hair wisping out in multiple directions. "Prison was just the tip of the iceberg for Pearletta Vee. She's going to pay in full for delivering drugs to Henry when he was on the road to healing. She'll lose her only child, just like we did."

I try to keep her talking. "Are you going to give me an overdose, like the others?"

"Yes, of course. What you had before was just a mild sedative. *This*"—she sets the gun down and picks up a long syringe—"is a special concoction that uses that Fentanyl they found at your mom's. It'll be my pleasure to call the cops when I 'find' your body outside your mom's trailer."

"And then you'll stop dealing?" I ask, slowly rising to my feet.

She picks up the gun and it bobs wildly, giving me some hope that she has no idea how to use it. "Hey—no sudden moves! And I don't know. I've developed a real skill in ridding this town of the dregs that are destroying it. This plan could be even farther-reaching than I'd thought. Since I control the drugs in this town, I could easily kill all the users in one fell swoop. Then it would just be a matter of tidying up loose ends, like Jelly Belly and Kyle. No one would ever suspect me—good gracious, I'm just the pharmacist's wife!"

She gives a cackle and I take my split-second opportunity, racing past her toward the door. It opens, and I run down the main stairs, focusing on the front door.

She starts screaming, her slow footsteps pounding behind me. "Stop her!"

Kyle's nowhere in sight. I pull the front door open and I've managed to get one foot out when he tackles me from behind, slamming my face into the wood porch. My vision blurs again.

The sudden roar of a familiar engine gives me hope. I squint up, trying to see if the driver is who I think it is.

Sure enough, the huge black truck barely slows, turning off the road and careening right into the yard. It continues to plow forward, crushing several wooden front porch steps as it jerks to an abrupt halt. Rosemary leans forward in the driver's seat, trying to get a glimpse of me, but Zeke Tucker blocks her view. He aims his weapon out the rolled-down passenger window, using the door as his shield.

"Get off her!" Zeke commands.

It takes Kyle a moment to act, but he finally pushes himself off me. I raise my head as much as I can and shout, "She's got a gun!"

Several police cars race to a halt behind the truck, and Zeke makes a hand motion. Cops pour out, weapons raised.

I struggle into a sitting position opposite Kyle. I really don't want to get caught in the middle of a firefight.

The screen door slams open, and the last person I expected steps out, his hands in the air.

Elmer Yates.

# 27

Mr. Yates looks disoriented, his eyes flicking from Kyle and me to the police. His hands remain in the air as he walks down the intact porch steps, then shimmies over the final bashed-in ones.

A police officer steps forward and ushers Mr. Yates toward his vehicle. Meanwhile, Zeke orders Kyle to come down from the porch.

Kyle shoots me a final hassled look, as if I'm the cause of all his problems, then follows instructions. I scoot back more, hoping I can jump the porch railing and get out of harm's way in case Matilda's about to make her grand entrance.

I try to warn Zeke. "Mrs. Yates is the one with the gun," I shout. "She's inside."

"You get down here," Zeke says.

Unwilling to take the stairs, which could place me in Matilda's sights, I stand and jump over the side railing, landing on a low bush below. I scramble to my feet and race to the driver's side of the truck.

Rosemary throws her truck door open, pulling me inside

like I weigh next to nothing. She slides into the middle of the driver's seat, making room for me, then reaches over and slams the door behind me.

"Ruby's okay," she says. "Fell a ways, but she landed right. Might've sprained her elbow, that's all."

I choke back my thankful tears. Never one to let a dramatic moment go to waste, Rosemary shushes me.

"She's coming out," she whispers.

Sure enough, Matilda Yates steps outside and slips her apparently empty hands into the air. She's quickly surrounded by police officers, who cuff her and troop her back to their vehicle.

I can't believe it. It was that easy.

Zeke turns to me. "Are you hurt?"

I rub at my face, which will probably be bruised from its run-in with the porch, but that's hardly anything earth-shattering. "I'm okay," I say.

"Okay. Ruby's told us quite a bit already." He peers out at the slanting roofline. "Girl's got a lot of guts, jumping down from there."

"She sure does," I say, also thinking of how Ruby put her life in danger to expose Mason's killer.

Zeke turns apologetic. "But we'll need your story, too. Have Rosemary bring you by the station on your way home. I know you need to decompress, but it's best if you tell us what happened while it's fresh in your mind."

"Your mom's already home," Rosemary adds.

"That's not home," I say.

Rosemary's lips pinch and she raises an eyebrow. Sensing trouble, Zeke unobtrusively slips from his seat to talk with Sheriff Biff, who's walking toward us.

Rosemary fixes me with a piercing stare. "Fine, then. She's back at the trailer. But, like it or not, she's still your mom."

At the police station, my purse is returned to me and I answer questions for a couple of hours. It sounds like Matilda has already given the cops an earful, most of it ranting about my mother's drug-dealing activities.

Zeke tells me Mr. Yates hasn't confessed to anything—in fact, he acted shell-shocked from the entire experience.

"He'll probably lose his pharmacist's license, won't he?" I ask. "That's too bad, when his wife admitted she used her husband's key to steal that Fentanyl from the hospital. And I never saw him once when we were being held at his house. He must've just gotten home—"

"I hate to tell you, but he knew," Zeke said.

"He *knew*? You're sure? I mean, he did taunt me about my mom's past at the funeral, but for him to know his wife was a drug dealer..."

"He knew," he repeats. "I've seen that look before. It's just like those moms who know their husbands are molesting their daughters. He knew she'd gone off the deep end, and he didn't try to stop her. In fact, he was probably on the same page, just unwilling to take the risks she did."

We sit in silence.

"In some weird way, there was a kind of logic to it," he reflects. "She would have continued getting drugs off the streets by killing the druggies and eventually, the dealers. Like a one-woman army."

"I'm not sure that Mason or Lacey's families would agree."

Zeke nods. "She'll be put away, that's for certain." He gives me a once-over. "You need to get home, Tess. Get back to your husband and daughter. If I need anything else from you, I'll know where to find you."

It's like someone's handed me the keys to my freedom. "You sure?"

"Don't even wait another day. I know your momma's back at the trailer, probably waiting to catch up. But you need your family right now. Take care of yourself, would you?"

He gives a flash of a smile, but thankfully stands and strides off before I completely lose my composure.

He's right. My time here is over. For once in her life, my mom's in the clear. And she's already proved she doesn't need my help to stay afloat.

I meet Rosemary in the hallway and we head out to her truck. The chrome bumper is only slightly dented after Rosemary's wild drive up the front porch steps.

"Thank you again," I say. "I'm sure Thomas'll want to pay for that damage."

"Now, how about you shut your mouth and stop being so humble, Tess Spencer. You just stopped a *killer*. I did next to nothing. I'm not taking your money."

As the wind whips through our open windows, loaded with the familiar, earthy scents of the mountains, I tilt my head back against the seat and let myself relax.

By the time Rosemary pulls into the trailer park, I know what I have to do.

Billy Jack peers out my mom's door as we drive up, then throws it open wide. "Come on in. She's been waiting for you."

I walk past Billy Jack with Rosemary trailing behind me. Mom's bustling around the kitchen, opening containers of Chinese food. When she sees me, she hurries to my side and folds me in a tight hug.

"You're okay! I could hardly make out what that detective was talking about—something about a kidnapping? And Ruby?"

"Long story," I say. "Mom, I wish I could stay and talk, but I really need to get on home. My friend Rosemary's heading out tonight, too." I gesture toward the bedroom she disappeared into.

"But honey, I know you must be exhausted. And Billy Jack picked us up some Wong's."

"I'll take some for the road. Awfully nice of Billy Jack to think of that, though." I glance into the living room, where he's watching a ballgame on TV.

"It was. Now, hold up a second. Your daddy told me he visited you?"

I can't get started down that rabbit-trail. "I don't want to talk about it. I need to get back to Thomas and Mira Brooke, and I see Billy Jack's looking out for you now."

Mom's eyes pool with tears. "Was it something I did? I had to hide with your daddy, Tessa Brooke. It was the only safe place from that Kyle feller."

"I understand." I give Mom a peck on the cheek. "I understand so much now. But the one thing I need you to understand is this: *I forgive you.*"

The power of those words rushes through me, purging all the torturous memories of my youth. It gushes into all the cracks my mom's neglect and addictions have created, filling them with a mercy that's not my own.

Mom's eyes well with tears, and I give her a hug. "I'll see you soon, I promise."

Rosemary tromps out, her suitcase and bag bulging even more than before. Even with her hair in a messy ponytail and her jeans a little on the loose side, Billy Jack can't help but give her an appreciative look.

She smiles down at him, sweet as molasses on cornbread. The queen beaming at her doting masses.

Then she turns to me, her face relaxing. "I'm going to hit the road. Thanks for the fun times."

Mom gives her a weird look, but Rosemary seems to be pretending Mom doesn't exist. She gathers her things and heads out the door with a flourish.

I feel immobile for a moment, but snap myself out of it. "Right. I'll double-check that I got everything. I've left the dirty sheets on the beds, Mom. But just one thing—when you take them to the Laundromat, if you see a guy in a fedora, promise me you'll stay well away from him, okay?"

⚜

On my way home, I stop by the hospital to check in on Ruby. When I step into the darkened room, Sally takes my hand.

"Thank you so much for finding her. I heard what you did."

"I hope they told you what a hero your daughter was. If she hadn't risked life and limb and gotten help…" My voice cracks.

Sally pats my hand. "Yes. And the best part is that she's clean, with no desire to go back to drugs."

"Worst rehab technique ever." Ruby croaks from her inclined bed. "Having to come to grips with your friend's death by overdose."

I recognize her deflection technique—making light of something that has pierced your heart. Walking to her bedside, I lower my voice so I don't wake the person snoring on the other side of the curtain.

"You make your own future," I say. "Promise you won't give up on yourself again. You're too strong for that." I take a long look at her bruised face and arms. Her elbow's in a splint and every movement makes her wince. "How did you get off that roof, or do I even want to know?"

She gives a partial smile. "I'm a good jumper, remember? That attic roof had quite a few gables. I was able to jump between them, then slide to the lower level. It was a big drop from the first story roof because it's quite high, but I made it.

Didn't quite nail the landing, but it all happened so fast."

I pat her dark curls. "Don't ever take a crazy risk like that again. Also, I'm so glad you took that crazy risk."

After saying our goodbyes, Ruby and I exchange phone numbers so we can text each other. Sally starts asking questions, but my energy is spent and I still have to drive home, so I give her a parting hug and beg off.

When I get to the SUV, I text Thomas to let him know I'm hitting the road. He calls me back immediately.

"I just got off the phone with Detective Tucker—he told me everything. He suggested I drive down and pick you up. Do you want me to?"

I consider it, but decide it's probably best if I have space to clear my head on the drive back. "No, thanks. I'm feeling okay, shockingly enough. But I'll tell you what you *can* do: put Mira Brooke to bed over at our house, so that when I wake up, the first thing I'll see is her beautiful face."

"Request granted," he says. "But when you walk in our door tonight, the first thing you're going to see is me, and I'm going to kiss you so long and so hard, you're going to forget which way is up."

I laugh. "I'll be counting on it."

# 28

A week after my return, Nikki Jo and I set up a belated celebration for Mira Brooke's second birthday. We decided to do it out on the patio. That way she can tumble around in the Spencers' well-groomed yard, play in her kiddie pool, blow bubbles, and eat popsicles to her heart's content.

I've invited my mom, and for the first time, I'm hoping she'll show up. Something's changed inside me. I want her to get to know Mira Brooke, even though it'll take quite a while before I feel comfortable letting her babysit.

Early this week, Thomas' brother Andrew arrived home, on break from college. He's a junior now, and as far as we can tell, he's still hoping to get into med school. This visit has been unique in that he hasn't yet had a girlfriend drop by, so we're hopeful he might actually be focusing on his studies.

I putter around the Spencers' bluestone patio, setting bright paper plates along the farmhouse table. Their back patio is like a shady oasis on hot summer days, with its curtained pavilion.

I wish Charlotte could be here. She's always had a soft spot for Mira Brooke, and we recently named her godmother to our daughter. Charlotte won't be flying in until next week. While I'm sure Bartholomew Cole will be anxious to catch up with her, I've already asked her over for coffee and chitchat once she settles back in at her large house in town.

Rosemary shocked me by accepting my invitation to Mira Brooke's party. I still feel guilty for asking her to probe around at Tranquil Waters, even though she promises it was just the excitement she'd craved. She mentioned that she's been checking in with Lacey's family every now and then. Something about the experience has definitely sobered Rosemary up—or maybe she's just less hyper now that she's kicked smoking for good.

Roger Spencer, my father-in-law, comes out with bright green plastic cups and hands them to me. "It's looking great. Nikki Jo's squeezing lemons for lemonade, and I'll have the meats ready soon." He walks over to his super-size grill and turns the hot dogs and burgers.

Mira Brooke is wearing her ruffled bathing suit, playing in the yard with Petey and the family dog, Thor. Thor is getting a bit long in the tooth, but that doesn't stop him from yipping every time he sees me, even though he knows exactly who I am.

Andrew saunters out, wearing Birkenstocks which are covered in paint splatters, mud, and grass stains. His older *Ocean's Eleven* T-shirt features a large picture of Brad Pitt, which is probably an inside joke, since Andrew is mistaken for Brad all the time.

He catches me looking at the shirt and grins mischievously. "I have an *Interview with a Vampire* shirt, too, if that's more your speed. Though word on the street has it you're more of a werewolf girl."

I turn to hide my blush. Seriously, why does Thomas have to share these things with his younger and far more immature brother?

He notices, and thankfully changes the subject. "Say, where is that brother of mine? Working on the weekend again?"

"He had a brief to finish writing, but he said he'd be home any minute."

Nikki Jo sweeps onto the porch, carrying two large pitchers. She gives Andrew's arm a light smack. "Get yourself inside and help me carry things out, young man. Your daddy nearly has the hot dogs and burgers done. Tess, I think someone's at the door."

I race through the kitchen and dining room and throw open the front door. My mom stands outside, examining Nikki Jo's flower-filled urns. She's had her hair colored so it's a uniform light brown hue, and she's wearing a dark purple shirt that makes her eyes look especially blue.

"You look great, Mom." I give her a kiss and hug. "Mira Brooke's out back."

I usher her inside, but the doorbell rings again. "You go right on through," I say, patting Mom's back.

I open the door again, only to find Rosemary standing outside. "I think Thomas is right behind me," she says.

"Doesn't he still drive that old silver car?"

"Somehow, he does." I hug Rosemary and take the gift she's brought for Mira Brooke. Today she's looking slightly more demure in a short denim skirt and loose green blouse, although her gold lace-up gladiator sandals add the glam touch I've come to expect.

I walk her back to the patio. Petey's settling Mira Brooke in her high chair, and Rosemary rushes over to give her chubby porcelain cheek a peck. Mira Brooke gives her a happy grin.

Rosemary turns. "Tess, she is positively the most delectable child I have ever seen."

Mom and Nikki Jo have fallen into a quiet conversation—I think it's about coleslaw recipes—and it's a relief to see them getting along. When Mom stayed with us the first couple of weeks after prison, she and Nikki Jo rarely saw eye-to-eye, especially on issues involving Mira Brooke. The few times I wound up playing tiebreaker, I had to side with Nikki Jo.

Andrew carries hot dogs and burgers over from the grill. He sets the plate on the table, his eyes sweeping toward Rosemary. As if prodded by some deeper instinct, Rosemary abruptly turns from Mira Brooke to meet his gaze.

Rats. I should've known this could happen. At the last meal we had, Andrew was checking out Charlotte. Now I can tell he's dialing up his swagger factor, striding toward Rosemary to introduce himself.

Thomas would not like this.

As if on cue, Thomas ambles over from the driveway,

joining us on the patio. I can tell from his glower that he didn't have a fun morning at work, and he doesn't even seem to notice Andrew hitting on Rosemary. He walks straight to me and gives me a peck on the forehead.

"Stinking habeas brief. Nothing but bogus claims."

I nod, as if I totally understand what he's talking about.

Nikki Jo hugs him and motions us all to the table. "Come and get it while it's hot, y'all!"

After prayer, as the dishes are passed around, Andrew starts questioning me about my latest adventure. I suspect he's trying to draw attention to himself, but I humor him and answer his questions.

"So, Tess, let me get this straight. You uncovered a drug dealer—and she was a woman? And a pharmacist's wife?"

"I didn't really uncover her. Let's just say she sort of threw herself in the spotlight."

"By kidnapping you and Ruby," Rosemary adds drily.

Andrew now fixes Rosemary with his full-on stare, the stare guaranteed to set most females quivering. "And if I heard right, you drove up to save them?"

"In my truck," she says, biting into her hot dog without one iota of self-consciousness.

"Crazy." Andrew might as well sit up and beg for attention, like Thor, who's expectantly positioned himself next to Petey's leg.

Thomas is still oblivious to the dynamic between Andrew and Rosemary, so he's definitely not in a good place right now.

I hope he snaps out of it before we bring out Mira Brooke's cupcakes.

Mom pipes up, her hamburger dripping ketchup onto the plate. "The sheriff stopped in to apologize. He said he always figured I wasn't involved."

Sure. He just needed me to prove it for him.

"How is Ruby?" Rosemary asks.

Mom answers for me. "She's all healed up and living with her momma for now, but she's filling out college applications." She beams and turns to me. "That reminds me, Tess, she said to tell you thanks. I don't know what for."

I smile, thankful that Ruby's story will have a happy ending, unlike Mason's.

Mom continues. "And they just arrested someone who goes by the name of Jelly Belly for dealing drugs. Isn't that the craziest name?"

"Sure is," I say.

After we finish eating and clean up the table, Nikki Jo carries out a huge plate of cupcakes. I help Mira Brooke blow out her two candles, then she promptly smears her cupcake all over her face.

My cell phone rings and I glance at the number. It's Diana, the social worker.

I hand Mira Brooke to her daddy and walk off the patio to talk. "Hello?"

"Hi, Mrs. Spencer. This is Diana. You had wanted updates on the situation with Brady. The home we placed him in temporarily wasn't a good fit, and he has no other family members nearby. I know your interest in the child, and I saw how he responded to your husband. Now, I'm sure you'll need some time to consider, but I thought I'd ask if you'd be interested in fostering?"

My world shifts a little. I picture those big blue eyes and that sad little face. I can't stand to see Brady shuttled into the foster system with complete strangers, when he does have a connection with Thomas and me.

"When do you need an answer?" I manage to ask.

"In two weeks. He'll be fine where he is until then. There are just circumstances beyond the family's control, and they will no longer be able to foster at that point."

"I'll talk to my husband and get back to you," I say.

"Thank you, Mrs. Spencer."

I take a moment, letting my eyes run over the delicious blue-greens of Nikki Jo's hostas. Everything feels so peaceful here, so right. The family's all together for a birthday celebration and the Spencer house is overflowing with love.

But what if there's someone else who should be in this family? A little boy who doesn't really know what *home* is?

Sliding my phone into my pocket, I walk toward the patio. Mira Brooke shouts, "Mama," and Thomas puts her down so she can toddle over into my arms. I plant a kiss on her curls and squeeze her tight. A tear escapes and drops to her cheek. She bats it away, laughing.

Thomas doesn't miss it. He stands and joins me. No one

pays attention, since Nikki Jo is pouring fresh rounds of coffee and Petey's bustling around, piling Mira Brooke's wrapped presents on the table.

Thomas pulls both of us into a hug, his eyes softening. "What's going on?"

"Brady." I'm so choked up, I can't elaborate.

My husband takes one long look at me. "He needs us," he says.

I nod.

Thomas takes a moment to think. Then he says, "Okay."

I can't believe I got to marry this man. We both know that fostering will not be a fast or easy process. It'll likely be fraught with issues and heartaches we couldn't possibly see coming.

But Thomas is with me, lending his strength, ready to catch me every time I fall.

I lean up and give him a long kiss.

Andrew whistles from the porch. My mom turns and smiles—a carefree smile, something I've rarely seen on her face.

Nikki Jo shouts, "You want some more coffee, Tess?"

I can't think of anything that could make this day better, even though I know Nikki Jo's strong java might keep me awake half the night. I grin. "Sure thing!"

Thomas slips his arm in mine, and we walk back to the family I was born to be a part of.

# Jane's Rhubarb Cake

1/2 cup butter

1 cup sugar

1 egg

1 cup sour milk

1 tsp vanilla

2 cups flour

1 tsp soda

1/2 tsp salt

2 cups rhubarb (cut up)

1/2 tsp cinnamon

1/4 cup sugar

(Preheat oven to 350 degrees.)

In a mixing bowl, cream butter and 1 cup sugar. Add egg and beat well. Combine sour milk and vanilla. Set aside. Combine flour, soda, and salt. Add alternately with milk mixture to the creamed mixture. Stir in rhubarb. Spread in a greased 9x13" pan. Combine 1/4 cup sugar and 1/2 tsp cinnamon and sprinkle on top of cake. Bake in a 350 degree oven for 35 minutes. Top with cool whip or milk topping (1 1/2 cup milk, 1/3 cup sugar, and 1 tsp vanilla in mixer).

# About the Author

**HEATHER DAY GILBERT**, a Grace Award winner and bestselling author, writes novels that capture life in all its messy, bittersweet, hope-filled glory. Born and raised in the West Virginia mountains, generational story-telling runs in her blood. Heather writes Viking historicals and Appalachian mystery/suspense. *Publisher's Weekly* gave Heather's Viking historical *Forest Child* a starred review, saying it is "an engaging story depicting timeless human struggles with faith, love, loyalty, and leadership." Find out more on heatherdaygilbert.com.

**You can find Heather online here:**

**Website:**

http://heatherdaygilbert.com

**Facebook Author Page:**

https://www.facebook.com/heatherdaygilbert

**Twitter:**

@heatherdgilbert

**Pinterest:**

https://www.pinterest.com/heatherdgilbert/

**Goodreads:**

www.goodreads.com/author/show/7232683.Heather_Day_Gilbert

**E-Mail:**

heatherdaygilbert@gmail.com

*If you enjoyed* Guilt by Association, *please leave a review on your online book retailer of choice or on Goodreads. Positive reviews encourage authors more than you know!*

*For all the latest on Heather's upcoming mysteries, please sign up for her author newsletter at* http://eepurl.com/Q6w6X.

Made in the USA
Coppell, TX
02 May 2020

24065506R00125